your story.

Tom Weakley

COVER PHOTO: Tommy is posing on top of the cement wall into which he will one day drive his father's brand new Packard.

Tom Weakley

—The Stories—

Highland Publications
Arlington, Vermont

HIGHLAND PUBLICATIONS
48 SCHOOL STREET
ARLINGTON, VERMONT 05250

COVER PHOTO OF TOMMY BY MIRIAM WEAKLEY MCCRAY

ILLUSTRATIONS BY BRUCE HISCOCK

FIRST PRINTING OCTOBER 2012

DESIGNED BY SPECTRUM DESIGN, BENNINGTON, VERMONT

MANUFACTURED IN THE UNITED STATES OF AMERICA

ISBN 978-0-615-70198-1
LIBRARY OF CONGRESS CONTROL NUMBER: 2012950097

For Barbara Ann Campbell Weakley,

the girl on the train

In memorium:

– Jack Lingenfelter   1929 - 2012

CONTENTS

AUTHOR'S PREFACE

Through the years when I told stories in public there was often a member of the audience who corralled me after the show to ask pretty much the same question: "Have any of your stories been published?" I gave the storyteller's stock answer that seldom satisfied: "Storyteller's publish by recording their stories." The questioner often appeared let down by my answer. Possibly they pictured a story they could see as well as hear. One they could hand off to a friend. Well, now they can.

When I thought to publish a short collection of the pieces that appealed to my readers as well as to me I discovered that several had not been recorded at all. And when I went to find a printed copy, they had been thought so little of that they had disappeared over the years (the copies, not the friends). Finding those I had recorded for sale was easy. Finding the others was a challenge.

Luckily storyteller Jeannine Laverty of Saratoga Springs, New York, had instructed her many followers to practice the stories aloud on cassette tapes in order to learn (not memorize) them. I had an extensive file of those and a well-maintained list of where to find each story. My professional transcriber, Christine Meyer, patiently (I suppose — I never watched her at work) typed out my every word and grunt on the original tapes resulting in printed copies I could then edit for this collection.

I quickly learned that the written word is a different animal from the spoken word. In performance I was free to pace the stage, lean forward in confidence, whisper asides, laugh, scratch myself and give in to all manner of buffoonery.

A word to those who might look for number 45 Prendergast Street in Jamestown as a family once did after listening to these stories. Our house was really 45 *Fourteenth* Street. It was suggested that Fourteenth Street sounded more like Manhattan than a town in Chautauqua County so I changed the name to honor the city's founder, James Prendergast.

There are many among you who will hear my voice when you turn these pages and for that we'll both be happy. For those who wanted to take the stories home in a book, I hope you'll be pleased that, after a little wait, I got around to it.

These 20 stories vary in length and in spirit, demonstrating, I hope, the range of emotions a good story can bring us. Some years back I was asked if I had a mission statement. I didn't. But, given a gun to my head, I'd have to say that I'd be content to look back on my life and find that we had come to a place where we could laugh and cry together.

ACKNOWLEDGEMENTS

Were it not for Jeannine Laverty neither this book nor my six CDs would have been published. In 1981 she graciously allowed me to join one of her early storytelling workshops though it was already full of participants.

Over the years my teacher Jeannine became my coach, my mentor and my dear friend. She continues to ask the right questions when I seek her counsel. All storytellers have been blessed who have put our work in her hands.

I was fortunate to find illustrator Bruce Hiscock between books so his vignettes could enhance these stories. Bruce read the entire collection and set out to illustrate the key moment in many of the stories. I am especially grateful for his compassionate heart, creative eye and steady hand with pen and ink.

Thanks also go to storyteller and musician Bill Harley who called my attention to children's use of the descending musical minor third interval in their calling to one another outside friends' houses. All this time I had thought it was the invention of kids on Prendergast Street.

These stories have been further shaped by the generous and on-going editorial skills of Joel Tibbetts, first readings and proofreading by Marilyn Houston, and Christine Meyer's word-for-word transcriptions of my recorded voice when original copies couldn't be found.

Jonah Spivack of Spectrum Design gathered the disparate elements of my original concept into an organic creation of which, like Willie's oak tree, anyone could be proud.

Finally I thank my many friends and colleagues in the storytelling community who have encouraged my efforts over the years. And the audiences who cried and laughed with me when we recognized ourselves in these stories.

ABOUT THE AUTHOR

Tom Weakley grew up in Jamestown, New York, and graduated from the Syracuse University School of Journalism in 1951. After serving in the United States Marine Corps during the Korean conflict he was on a train headed for Seattle with the expectation of settling in Japan when he met Barbara Campbell, a commercial artist, in the dining car. She was on her way to Yellowstone National Park to do some sketching. They spent a day together, exchanged addresses and within six months they had fallen in love by mail. Tom returned to the East to take a position as an editor on a trade publication in New York City. They were married and moved to Vermont to open a successful candle-making business and raise their two children, Christopher and Margaret. After retirement Tom began writing and telling stories before adult and

fam... the country. Tom has been a
mai... he National Storytelling Fes-
tiva... recorded six CDs of stories.
Bar... Arlington, Vermont, where
the... ...s of the Taconic Mountains.

family audiences around the country. Tom has been a mainstage performer at The National Storytelling Festival in Tennessee and has recorded six CDs of stories. Barbara and Tom live in Arlington, Vermont, where they enjoy sweeping views of the Taconic Mountains.

TWO PICKPOCKETS

Young fellow lived over in Brattleboro. Had a great job. He was his own boss and he loved the work. It got him out in the fresh air at sporting events, brought him to cultural performances over in New Hampshire and down to the Five Colleges in Massachusetts. He attended the Rutland State Fair every year as well as county fairs around New England, all part of the job. He was good at what he did and he prospered.

He was a pickpocket.

It occurred to him that if he did this well in little old Brattleboro, imagine what it would be like in the big city. So he moved to Burlington. Up there are all kinds of things that aren't in Brattleboro — college sporting events, for instance. And a marina.

One hot summer's day he was on Church Street in Burlington where all those little boutiques and bistros are. Many shoppers had gone home to sit by their air conditioner or had gone for a swim in the lake. He had about decided to go home himself when it occurred to him that… his wallet was missing.

He spun around to look up and down the street, where he saw a young woman walking away from him faster than she had a right to on such a hot day. He caught up with her and accused her of stealing his wallet, to which she tearfully confessed.

She gave him back his wallet, but even better, she agreed to share a pint at one of those little pubs. "There isn't anybody on the East Coast," he told her, "could touch me like you did without me knowing it. You're good. How about you and me joining forces? If we teamed up, we could take in more than twice what one of us makes now."

She was persuaded and they went into business together, occasionally helping people squeeze in and out of their cars on the Lake Champlain ferry to New York. One morning over breakfast downtown he offered another proposal. "Suppose you and I were to get married… now wait, just hear me out, okay? Supposing we got married and we had a baby… wait a minute!… and we have a baby, see. Now, all the genes from my fingertips and all the genes from your fingertips would all be blended into the fingertips of that baby. By the time that child graduated high school you and I could move to France and he would just send checks to us once a month!"

Long story short — they did get married and soon she was bearing a child and her time came to give birth. They called the midwife and the midwife delivered a beautiful baby boy. But that baby had a strange malady. When that child was born, his little arm was all drawn up tight against his chest, his little fist closed tight. No amount of massaging or warm baths or pulling away, first by the midwife and then the doctors and nurses, could budge that little arm.

Now, to parents like you and me that would be bad enough; but to these people, it was their whole future. It was his pocket-picking hand and they spared no expense to correct it with no success.

Finally, they heard about a doctor in Boston who was a great diagnostician. With their last few dollars, they took the bus to Boston, walked over to Children's Hospital and into the doctor's office. The nurse showed them into the examining room. "Put your baby on the table," she said, "the doctor will be right in."

The doctor came in. After several minutes of questions he confessed: "In all my years of practice, I've never heard of anything like this." To begin his examination he reached in his pocket to pull out his pocket watch. With his other hand he put his fingertips on the baby's wrist. While measuring the heart beat he said to the parents: "See how animated he is. Why, I think he's admiring my watch."

To confirm it he let his watch dangle at the end of its gold chain and slowly swung it over the baby's body. Those little eyes followed that gold watch back and forth, back and forth, until... slowly the little arm began to move away from the body and reach up toward that swinging gold watch until the little hand opened and out fell the midwife's wedding ring.

ADRIFT ON THE
ALFALFA SEA

She saw herself by this time the unofficial folk teller of Mount Ira — her world a continuum of stories about people and their memories, a jumble of truth and invention. Old age brought the soft footsteps of dementia and her belief that all the waters of the world were somehow connected one to another. So even as she sat on the toilet seat there in Mount Ira, she felt herself to be suspended some five to six inches over what had once been the billows of the great Pacific Ocean. In some this might have invoked fear, but for her it was as if all of the stories in the world were thrust into bottles and thrown into the sea. And if she were patient, if she were to live long enough, those stories would, one by one, flow out of the kitchen pump in Mount Ira.

Her storied life began with memories of her own childhood. Not ones that she recalled happening, but ones she remembered because they had been told so often. She didn't learn stories at her mother's knee, but from her father as she balanced on the tub's edge watching him shave.

"Jean, I remember," he told her, "the time you fell through the boards covering the well over to the Thrall farm and I jumped in to save you but there was no water in the well to save you from. Everyone laughed for years about that.

"Do you remember the time you snuck the strawberries away from the dinner table and carefully hid them under the living room rug to be eaten later, only to forget all about them?"

On other days he told her about cows that talked to him while they were being milked. Or the hired hand who turned into a goat, and what his grandfather told him about where the new moon came from. All this spoken through lips twisted first left, then right, up and down through the sweet-smelling white foam on his rubber face.

It was the same comforting scent of shave cream that the hardware salesman used when her mother rented him the room next to hers the year Jean graduated from high school. It was cash money for her mother every other week when he passed through that patch of Iowa. He was little more than a high school graduate himself, at his first job, and intoxicated with the American dream of a house and car and someone to share it with.

For the better part of that year his whispered endearments on the hanging porch swing made his dream her own. She saw him as her way out of Mount Ira. He asked for her parents' approval which was granted and they were married before planting season the following spring.

They stayed in her family home. "Just for a while," he told her, "until we get something ahead." She liked having someone close to her who had never heard the stories. They flowed out of her, one story reminding her of the next. He seemed to like the stories, but his eyes wandered sometimes when she was but half way to the end. Stories began to come unbidden, ones her father hadn't told her, sometimes as she washed dishes or hosed down the apron behind the stanchions after the morning milking. She kept a bunch of old milk receipts on the bathroom windowsill to write on as she lay soaking in the tub in water she would later imagine once lapped on the verge of tropical lagoons.

Then one morning in November she awoke to find him packing. "Hardware," he told her, "is no longer the product of the future."

"What is?" she asked from her pillow.

"I don't know," he said, "but Iowa isn't where it's going to take hold. Whatever is coming next I want to be on the ground floor out on the coast."

"On the coast?"

"California," he said. "The future is being invented out there and they'll need the sales know-how of people like me. I'll be there to get in on the ground floor. Don't worry," he said. "I'll get something ahead and I'll send for you."

By 9:45 that morning they were waiting for the bus at the crossroads. What neither of them knew was that he had already sent something ahead, and it was growing inside of Jean as the bus carried him down Boundary Road and out of her life.

She got one card from him, from Salt Lake. It showed bathers eating lunch from a card table riding the placid water.

If he ever got to the coast, she never heard.

His name was Robert and with the hope that lives within the hearts of storytellers Jean named their child Roberta. Then it was her daughter who heard the stories — of second-prize ribbons at the fair, fathers in the well, girls with red caps, strawberries under the rug, why milk is white, and why birds' nests are round.

Roberta grew to young womanhood and, though she didn't go to the coast, did one day take the bus to the city and a world of her own.

In the years after her daughter left Jean took her stories to shut-ins and to the bereaved like word casseroles. She carried stories to the abandoned and the left-behind, some of whom, after her visits, she thought probably deserved it. The old, the very old, listened, still as stones, until their eyes closed against the light when she would sit nearby and give them the gift of silence.

After the tractor accident claimed her father, the livestock and equipment was sold off piecemeal. Her mother refused to sell the farm, the only home she'd known since she was married. She lived another eight years. The land was leased for corn, haying, and alfalfa.

For a time Jean was paid a small sum to tell stories in schools along the bus route. As she came to look forward to the money she began to worry that her talent mightn't last as long as she did. What would be first to go, she wondered. The voice? The stories? Maybe her memory. If I can just concentrate, she thought, maybe I can postpone its coming. As one corn harvest followed the next her stories became confused with one another and eventually with her everyday life. She was invited to the schools less and less — eventually not at all.

The RFD carrier was first to miss her when her box was not emptied. The county visiting nurse phoned Roberta.

Jean lay in her bed, back to the wall with its familiar paper, her knees drawn up, her arms hugging her breasts as if, by making a wreath of herself, she could attach the end of the story to the beginning and it would come out right.

Suddenly there was Roberta — bringing her beef consomme and crackers. She had also brought her husband. A man, the old woman thought, not likely to go to the coast on her. And they brought her granddaughter. "Oh," said the old woman to the child, "I'm glad to see you're big enough not to fall through the cracks."

Later the child came into the shade-drawn room to lie on the bed with her grandmother, to tell her of things from beyond the rolling seas of alfalfa outside the window. She spoke of lost cats, dying elms, and what is really inside lima beans. She told her of the friend who lived in her bureau drawer at home. But then the door opened and Roberta scooped up the girl from the bed.

"Grandma needs to rest," she whispered as she carried the child from the room.

Jean lay in the gloaming, hearing the child's stories once again. Something in them opened the sluice gate on memories from her own journey. Never before, she thought, have I strung all my stories together like beads on a necklace. Once she saw them all in place it told a lovely story.

She saw the door open. It was her son-in-law. She motioned for him to come and sit by her. When he sat down the raft on which she lay rocked in the water. She saw all the beads together in not quite a circle but almost — strawberries, oak leaves, lima beans, even a bus. "Beads," she whispered.

"What?" asked the man. He bent to hear her, rocking the raft once more.

"I have a story," she said.

"What did you say?"

She opened her eyes. Her hand fluttered to the top of his head to rest there trembling.

"You've been gone a long time," she said to him. "Why didn't you send for me?"

Now the raft carried her gently across the road, onto the swelling alfalfa-colored sea, its waves flecked with foam like deep purple shaving cream. When the raft crested the billows she could see the farmhouse on the shore. If I had a card table, she thought, I could eat lunch out here. She sought to taste the water on which she floated. If it is salt it will be the sea, she thought, but she was too tired to bring her hand back out of the water.

At the end she felt herself inside a bottle and floating on the alfalfa sea. She drifted westward until one day out on the coast where he was digging a well for their new home he lifted her bottle from the bubbling water. She opened her eyes to him. "I have such a story to tell you," she whispered.

"Let me hear it, sweetheart," he said. And he laid his shovel to one side.

SLEEPING OUTSIDE EDEN

The train to Washington was crowded and the two men had to settle for seats across the aisle from each other. The older man was slender with white thinning hair, steel-blue eyes above a prominent nose and full lips through which he passed a dried apricot. He held out a crumpled paper bag of dried fruits across the aisle, shaking it to draw the younger man's attention. "Take some, Edgar," he said, "but save some for lunch." The younger man took a handful.

"Pop, it's not too late to get a place to stay overnight."

"I didn't bring a change of clothes," said the old man.

"Just for overnight. When you're in your eighties you shouldn't be trying to do all this in one day."

"I can't sleep away from home."

They chewed in silence as passengers passed juggling cardboard trays of coffee and Danish. The old man leaned over between passing jugglers. "Just when did he go overseas?"

"November of '68... just before Thanksgiving." The memory remained painfully fresh for Edgar. Just the year before he had talked the boy out of going to Canada. They had embraced — something that hadn't happened in a long time. He touched his chin remembering the roughness of the boy's bristle against his cheek. He was not yet a man even as we said goodbye, he realized. Trains and train stations still made him ill at ease. He wouldn't be on this train today except for the boy's grandfather whose idea it was to commemorate what would have been his grandson's fortieth birthday. He had talked of little else since the memorial was completed four years before.

"I wonder," he said to the old man, "whether he ever got my last letter."

"What was in it?"

"Memories mostly. How I regretted that fathers and sons can't see eye-to-eye just at the time it's important they do."

In Washington it was the old man who led the way, map in hand, through traffic on unfamiliar avenues. His son followed, alert to cars skirting the Lincoln Memorial. He hurried to catch up with his father who waited for him at the curb. From the corner they overlooked a stretch of green just below. "There it is." The old man pointed to what resembled a wound in the earth. "Come on." He moved along a curving path that intersected the embankment.

"I don't know if I want to go down there, Pop. You go; I can see it from here."

The old man turned around. "I just want to look on it, Edgar, to stand up close. Come on."

"Pop — he's not there."

"So? Where is he? Do you know?" He pointed back up the slope. "Do you know where he is? I can't speak for you — do what you have to do. This," he said, "is what I have to do." With that he resumed his descent.

Edgar followed at a distance, hands in his pockets. As the path reached the bottom of the slope, it curved toward an open, grassy area beyond. Three bronze larger-than-life figures stood beside the walkway. Young men, their eyes older by decades than they, gazed across what might have been a small meadow. There lay the black granite wall maybe a man and a half high at its apex and slowly giving way toward its ends like a buried sword working its way to the surface. Visitors lingered along the length of the wall, strolling, reaching out to touch names, comforting one another, lifting children to see, laying flowers and mementoes at the base.

As they approached, Edgar gripped his father's elbow.

"Look," he whispered.

He gestured toward a rumpled man facing the monument. The man's hands and fingers danced in fluid motions reflected from the surface of the wall on which his mirrored image was scarred by the letters chiseled there. A red bandana flashed between his shoulder-length hair and the collar of his fatigue jacket. A medal dangled from the pocket flap.

Near the path stood a pedestal with a book on it. The old man referred to it to learn which panel to look for. His fingers ticked off the panels from left to right. When he found the panel he counted in whispers as his hand ran down the lines. He stopped counting. His finger followed his gaze across the line of etched letters, then stopped.

"There he is," he whispered. He stroked the letters with his fingertips. He looked for his son, only to find him looking away, toward the entrance. The old man called gently, "Come over here." Edgar stood his ground.

The old man shuffled closer to the wall. With a self conscious glance down the walkway he rested one arm against the wall and leaned forward to press his lips to the name, the granite warm on his mouth. He stepped back, glanced toward his son, then moved slowly down the pathway to his right, reading names at random.

Edgar had noted, in spite of himself, where the old man had paused, where his hand had gone down the wall and now, as he followed his father, he was drawn to that panel. Like others, it was ornamented with memories: a fragment of blue taffeta near the name of a woman, a well-hugged vintage teddy bear with one button eye, a photograph curling in the sun. He uncurled it: a snapshot of a 1965 Plymouth Fury. Only then did he let his gaze fall to the spot where the old man had laid his fingers. There was his boy.

He traced each letter in turn with his finger. He read the names nearby. Names, he knew, were listed in the order of their death. They must all have been together at the end, or very close by. As he lifted his gaze on the mirrored surface he came face to face with his son: he had aged, his hair was gray and thinning, his face sagged under the eyes, but he looked much the same; no mistaking him. He closed his eyes against the vision. Leaning forward ever so lightly, he rested his head against the mirrored granite. The names, he thought, all our children.

Edgar pressed his cheek full against the warmth of the wall. From deep within came a moan. He collapsed against the wall — sliding over the unyielding names — their chiseled letters reaching for his face.

Again — a cry torn from deep within his loins from deep within, to rage from his mouth — from his mouth like a small animal crying in the darkness caught in the grip of another and crying. As he slumped down the granite face the names reached for his cheek: guttural names like Gaertner and Krueger, bright brittle names like Kimball and Proski; olive-skinned names of Paladino and Galati, homely names of Barber and Sawyer, rhythmic names of Morales and Romero and all while the cries of a young animal, crying like an animal caught in the jaws of the jungle.

Just before his knees touched the walkway, arms found him and caught him, cradling him in their embrace. He turned his face into the arms and let his heart have its way. Through choking sobs he cried, "Oh Pop, oh Pop!" The grip tightened as he was rocked amid the comforting fragrance of tobacco stained breath, the smell of clothes worn in honest labor. He relived the night as a child when he had had the earache and Pop had puffed warm smoke into his small ear. He could feel it yet, the pain in his ear, the smell of the tobacco — how real the sensation though his father had not smoked in years, and yet something of him was still in this coat... in this... this rough... coarse... coat.

He opened his eyes to stare at the Purple Heart that had been pressing into his ear. And within the collar of the fatigues, a flash of red. He looked into the face of the Vet. He struggled to his feet. The old man rushed up to help as best he could, to brush him off. The Vet, now relieved of duty, moved down the walkway, the old man calling after him, "Thank you!"

The men gathered their thoughts to remind themselves of where they stood before turning to walk down the rest of the walkway and up the curving path to the street. They sat in silence in the back of the cab on the way to the train. Turning to his father, Edgar said, "He spoke to me."

"Who spoke to you?"

"The man with the bandana. 'Gonna' be all right,' he told me. I could smell his breath when he talked." He stopped short of telling the old man everything.

"I loved him, Pop, I hope he knew that."

The old man looked out his window. "Family knows."

"Just the same, I told him so in that last letter; I told him right out." He turned his eyes away from the old man. "I hope he got it."

Once the train was underway, the old man groped in his coat pocket to pull out the rumpled bag of what remained of the dried fruit.

"It's time to sell the business," the old man said.

"Do we have to talk about it now?"

"It's past time for talking," said the old man. "It's time now to sell. Sell, get married again. Live — dance

— sing — tell jokes — go to China — live! Live! It's too late for me, but not for you."

A rush of tenderness warmed the old man with desire to hold his son close again, to comfort him in his rediscovered loss, as if, with a touch, he could take something of it on himself... absorb it in his old bones. He reached over to put his cool, dry hand atop his son's hand on the seat. It lay there cool, dry skin and bones, long fingers unmoving, not gripping, just being there; cool and dry before retreating. Neither man looked right or left.

The son spoke, "I wish now I had brought something to leave there."

The old man felt tired. It was a satisfied tiredness like at the end of the biggest day of the season at the store. And, he was hungry. He turned his attention to the last of the dried fruit. He crumpled the bag in one hand and set the fig between his teeth with the other. His tongue moved each dry morsel between his teeth. He heard as well as felt each soft seed crunch in his jaws. He tilted his seat back to rest his head against the paper-covered headrest and closed his eyes. He thought about this man riding next to him: closing the store, coming all this way from home to be sure he'd be all right. He had loved him as a boy, and now that he was a man — it wasn't something a man thought about much. He took it as a given. But he did love him. He's a good son, a good man. And some day, he promised himself, when the time was right, he would have to tell him so.

THE RASPBERRY AFFAIR

Visitors who wander up Route 100, the backbone of Vermont, and get lost exploring back roads, stand a chance of coming across the elongated village of Silver Springs. Black-shuttered white clapboard houses are strewn like stones on either side of a rocky stream. The town is hemmed in by hillsides so steep that sunshine warms the porch of the general store only four hours a day in mid-winter. Shading the porch on the east is Mount Holly and on the west by Cussed Hill. A cracked and fragmented marble sidewalk bounds the road on the east where it passes Bacon's Store. Children gather mornings on the porch of the store to await the yellow bus that will wind its way to the school over in Mount Holly village.

At the turn of the Twentieth Century the Silver Springs were noted for stimulating and, some said, curative powers. Canadians joined New Yorkers returning to the springs each summer to bathe and imbibe what local folks called "that smelly water!" Today weed-filled bath pools mark the remains of the rambling old wooden hotel at the north end of town. The brick bottling plant still stands at the other end, but the water is no longer bottled.

The lost tourist is rewarded by strolling what best resembles a movie set that might have been erected to film the New England values of a free and noble people. But behind the lilac bushes and lace curtains dwell villagers with well-honed skills at divining the lives of their neighbors on the off chance that their troubles are worse than one's own.

Townspeople hold that their neighborly concerns are driven more by compassion than curiosity. Still, once or twice a year, Pastor Betty from Mount Holly Methodist makes a stab at quelling rumors, half truths and assorted chatter about this one or that one. "It's alright," she says, "if you say so-and-so had an accident and needs our prayers. It is borderline gossip if you ask where the accident occurred. But then it is a sin to ask, 'What was she doing over there?'" thereby closing the door on any incentive to mention the accident at all. While no one argues that there is no merit in being told of another's joy, their probing for details about others' troubles, both random and self-inflicted, allow them to know whether there is an unexpressed call for help, for consolation, shared bitterness or, at the very least prayers, which, to be effective, need the full story. In short, discussing one's neighbors is as accepted as serving fresh venison out of season. Take, for example, what has come to be called The Raspberry Affair.

The general store owner, Rawley Bacon, grew up outside Silver Springs on his father's subsistence farm the other side of Mount Holly. Rawley first raised eyebrows when he courted young Emily Safford, the daughter of the last family ever to bottle water from the Silver Springs. Townspeople couldn't figure why young Emily would be attracted to this hard-working farm boy she met when he delivered eggs to her mother. He didn't have anything to bring to their union except a small flock of Rhode Island Reds, and his disarming innocence. To the further consternation of her mother, he was seven years her senior. But they weren't to be denied; they drove over to Rutland and got married.

First they lived upstairs in the big white house her daddy had built next to the store. The young couple shared the house with her mother until she died and left all the property to Emily. Rawley took over the store working sixty hours a week. He put in the first and only gas pump in town. And when the post-mistress retired, closing the post office in her home, Rawley and his brother turned a corner of the store into a post office.

But the one thing they thought they could accomplish on their own didn't happen. Emily could not become pregnant. To the townspeople she looked fertile enough. Her pink skin was pulled taut over every melon-like feature of her body. Her fingers seemed just made to push into that yielding dough for the sweet buns she put in the oven every morning.

Rawley and Emily were a couple in a time and place when you just didn't go and ask for help for that.

Nowadays you might go to the clinic in Ludlow. It was suggested they consider it to be God's will. That was a bitter pill for Emily. This was the one thing she wanted the most of anything in her whole life. It weakened her faith. She was a woman who believed that her god had promised good to all the faithful. When she looked back on those years of her failure — because she saw it as her failure — she thought there was something that she must have done wrong. While Emily grieved her disappointment, Rawley was undergoing a change of his own.

Rawley was looking around the store at this time and not seeing challenges any more. Here he was a man who, for ten straight years, had done the same thing, sold the same cans of kerosene, same work gloves, same bread, same eggs. He took to brooding about it, asking himself: Is this it? Then late one spring day in Rawley's life when he was thinking such thoughts, into his store came Dora Bliss.

Dora Bliss was selling her daddy's raspberries and when she bent over that crate of berries her tee shirt opened to set free any constraint on the smooth flesh of small breasts that inspired Rawley's palms to close and open with a life of their own. When she straightened up he found himself looking into the face of this comely young woman.

Here she'd been, he thought, coming in for the past ten years; he'd no doubt been looking over her head since she was nine. But now, Rawley, he starts pushing raspberries. What berries Rawley didn't sell honest he took to eating out of hand like peanuts just so every day Dora Bliss will have to come back and bend over that basket full of Soft. Round. Ripe. Juicy. Berries.

Then came the plums. Old man Bliss's plums had always been a bit on the sour side but Rawley took to telling folks that he read in a magazine as to how sour plums was good for the arthritis, which everybody in town complained they had. Then cucumbers. Then corn and tomatoes, squash, right up through apple time. Rawley began to think it was providence because otherwise who would have known twenty years before to plant that stand of Macintosh trees right up there on the Bliss farm and then send this girl down with those lovely Macs to be packaged in the back of his store?

Dora Bliss began coming in the evenings, to transfer those apples into little half-peck paper bags, and staying longer than it really would take to do that. Townspeople asked themselves afterwards: how could such a thing ever get started, the store being right next to the house as it was? The popular conjecture had it that Emily spent most of her time in the kitchen and the kitchen was on the other side of the house. Nobody really knew how long this went on until late one afternoon Dora Bliss came into the store. She carried a crumpled paper hankie. Her eyes were red.

"Hello, Dora."

"Hello, Rawley."

"You're dressed up. You been to Rutland?"

"Been over to Ludlow."

"Ladies' Aid? I thought they met on Tuesdays."

"Been to see Doctor Russell."

"Oh, I'm sorry. Not feeling well?"

She sighed and leaned up against the counter gazing at the man in the white bib apron they had spread beneath them those evenings in that apple-scented room.

"Rawley," she told him, "Doctor Russell says I am in the family way."

"You're in the what?" Rawley backed away from the counter.

"I'm going to have a baby," she said.

"Have a baby," he breathed.

"Some time in July."

"July," he said, suddenly unfocused.

"I'm going to have this baby, Rawley."

"Aw, sweetie, let's just stop and think." He lifted a shaking hand to his mouth.

"I thought all the way home," she said, her tears falling anew, her mouth contorted as she forced the words. "I'll have it. I'm going to have it. I can't do anything else."

"Yes!" he surprised himself with the force of his voice. "Yes, there are things that can be done. I just need some time to think and make…"

Dora regaining something close to composure, spoke the words with regret. "I will have the baby. But I'm not going to keep it. I'm not going to look on it."

"Sweetie, there are things we can do. You can do."

"Oh, stop it, Rawley. I know what I'm doing. My heart is set on the Rutland School of Cosmetology. I'm starting my life over. You can, too. Doctor Russell will find me a place in the unwed mothers' home in Burlington." She pulled a napkin from the dispenser on the counter and turned toward the door. "Goodbye, Rawley," she said. With the bang of the screen door Rawley came to himself. My God, he thought, if that girl tells even one person in this town she might as well go over to Mount Holly and shout it from the church steeple. I got to get to Emily.

Rawley closed early, turned off the lights, went out the back door. He jumped off the loading platform, ran across the driveway, around the house, up the back stoop and into the kitchen where Emily was punching down the dough for the next day's sweet buns. He pulled out a kitchen chair by the table. He sat to lay his head on the oil cloth, sobbing like a child. Stopping only to catch his breath he told his wife everything.

Emily stopped in mid-punch of the dough and stood looking straight ahead.

When he had finished his story she told him. "Go to bed, Rawley. We'll talk about it in the morning."

When Rawley came down for breakfast there was no smell of sweet buns. Emily stirred scrambled eggs in the skillet with a wooden spoon. She pushed half the eggs onto his plate and half on hers. She looked straight at him and said, "Rawley, that baby is most likely the baby I've been looking for all my life. Now, the fact that God has seen fit that Dora Bliss should bear it, I'm just going to have to lean on His understanding. But Rawley, if Dora doesn't want that baby, I do!"

There weren't enough tongues in all of Silver Springs to wag at the Raspberry Affair. Up and down Route 100 went the story. The baby's mother signed her agreement. It remained only for the baby to arrive.

For Rawley, it had the effect of a governor's reprieve! To him it appeared the best of all possible worlds. By Emily's lights he'd done just the thing she had wanted done. He became giddy at the thought of becoming a father. One morning he stood in the middle of the henhouse awash in tears at what he saw as God's grace. He fell to his knees to pledge all of next year's egg profits to the Mount Holly Methodist Church.

Emily fussed and fretted every day. She changed her sewing room into a nursery. She painted, arranged and rearranged bundles of diapers and little cotton coveralls that she'd ordered out of one of Rawley's store books.

The baby was born and an excited Emily couldn't wait to get her hands on that baby. They drove up to

Burlington to sign the final papers and came home with a baby girl in a basket. Rawley hopped out of the car to reach for the basket. "Here, I'll carry it in," he said.

"No," Emily said. "That's all right — not heavy."

All afternoon Rawley tried to hold the baby. "No, sshh, she's just gone to sleep."

Rawley wanted to feed her. "No, I'm not sure," she said, "I don't know but the milk might be too hot."

All day went by and Rawley hadn't yet held his little girl. In the morning he came down all eager to get started fathering. When he entered the kitchen Emily was standing at the stove stirring scrambled eggs. She spoke without turning around. "Rawley, I need to know something."

"What is it?" he asked.

"Does Judge Williams have a copy of the adoption papers?"

"You know he does, Emily."

She turned off the stove. She turned around to point the egg-covered spoon at him. "Rawley Bacon," she said, "I want you out of this house by 5 o'clock tonight."

"What are you saying, woman?"

"I want you out. I'm taking the baby over to Mabel Hulett's for the day and when I get back I want you gone. Take what belongs to you, but I don't ever want to hear your footstep in this house again."

That was thirteen, fourteen years ago. Emily borrowed money on the house and bought two gas ovens which she put into her kitchen to bake sweet buns and pies for the store over in Mount Holly. She got paid sometimes in provisions and if there was more left over she got cash.

Rawley has lived ever since upstairs over the store. After two or three incidents early on he had to put a restraining order on Dora's father, but the business pokes along much as it used to in the old days. Townspeople stop by for eggs and kerosene and work gloves.

Tourists who stumble onto Silver Springs might see that little girl sitting on the porch of that big white house right next to Bacon's Store. Emily named her Dorothy (gift of God), Dolly for short. If she isn't there, she's most likely in the store sitting on a stool behind the counter passing the time of day with the man in a big white apron. Out behind the store Rawley put in a raspberry garden. It belongs to Dolly. He thinks she might get a prize at the Rutland Fair some year for those berries. Next September he says he's going to take her and the berries to Rutland. Dora Bliss married a young man she met at the School of Cosmetology. Together they have a practice in a suburb of Albany, New York.

Town talk has it that every year on Dolly's birthday Emily has the girl send a birthday card to her natural mother. People say that over the years Dolly has been disappointed that she's never been answered by her mother. And on those occasions Emily beckons the girl to her side; she gives her a bosomy hug and reminds her that all good things come to those who have faith and are willing to wait.

DIRECTIONS

All approaches to Vermont are, by definition, beautiful, but the approach from the west brings one through picturesque Old Bennington with its stately black- shuttered white clapboard homes. Visitors pass the wedding cake Old First Church, the hillside cemetery where Robert Frost rests, the stone-faced Bennington Museum with its collection of Grandma Moses originals, then down the hill by the Hemmings Motor News Sunoco station, the first place you can reasonably stop to ask directions.

One summer morning a retired midwestern couple maneuvered their large motor home under the canopy of Hemmings Sunoco and beckoned to Bucky Grimm, a self-appointed town greeter. Since his retirement (he was an undertaker), Bucky has taken to hanging around Hemmings to make his knowledge of county roads available to visitors. The driver beckoned to Bucky. "I wonder if you can give us some directions," he called out. Bucky shuffled his way toward the motor home. "We're looking for The Candle Mill in East Arlington," said the driver.

Through cracked lips outlined with tobacco stains, Bucky cleared his rusty throat: "What you do is, you go back out here onto West Main (he pointed) and at the first light, go left onto Ben Mont. Then at the (his lips moved to count) second street make a right..." The driver nodded to acknowledge each turn while his wife, riding shotgun, wrote it down on a notepad. In the end the driver thanked him and drove off.

Fifteen minutes later here comes this same big motor home into Old Bennington, past the white clapboard houses with black shutters, past the wedding cake church, the Robert Frost cemetery, the Museum and pulled under the canopy of the Hemming Motor News Sunoco station, the driver mad as hell!

He yelled over to Bucky, "What do you mean sending us around in a damned circle? We followed your directions to the letter and wound up back here where we started from!"

"Well," said Bucky, "before I invested too much time in you I wanted to see could you follow directions."

THE METHODIST COMMUNION

On a rainy Sunday morning, some time back, while serving as a deacon in our small Vermont church, I misspoke a word in the middle of a communion service and have yet to forget it.

Ours is a "Federated Church," serving Methodists and Congregationalists in town. The incident in question occurred during the pastorate of David Andrews, a Congregational minister. During a previous meeting of the deaconate he had told us that our Methodist members wanted occasionally to be served communion according to the Methodist tradition. We had not done that since my wife, Barbara, and I had attended that church so I didn't know what he meant.

The Methodist protocol called for those in the pews to come forward in an orderly way to kneel at an altar rail to be served the elements before returning to their seats. In the Congregational tradition, as I knew it, the ushers brought a small tray of bread cubes to pass up and down each pew and, at a word from the pastor, the bread was eaten "in unison." Same thing with the juice.

Rev. Andrews reminded us, "Our church doesn't have an altar rail so people will come down the aisle to stand at the foot of the steps leading up to the altar. The space will hold a row of maybe eight, ten people at a time." He enlisted Clyde Dunlap, a life-long Methodist, and me, a Congregationalist, to assist him in serving the elements.

I should tell you a little about Clyde Dunlap who, alas, is no longer among us. Clyde, a taciturn man, had been a member of this church since his baptism. He said little and hesitated to speak other than good of any man, but, when he did, measured his judgments with compassion. Clyde was a carpenter and a builder — of homes, farm buildings, sap houses. By the time of the Sunday in question Clyde had retired to focus on his love of cabinetry.

"Here's how we'll do it," said Rev. Andrews. "I'll

offer the plate of bread to each person lined up at the foot of the altar. As they take it I'll say to each one, 'This is Christ's body, broken for you.' Then I'll move to my left to the next person. Now Tom," he said, "I want you to come along after me carrying the small cups of juice. As you offer it to each communicant you will say, 'This is Christ's blood shed for you.'" He turned to Clyde. "Clyde, you'll follow Tom carrying a tray on which each person can put their empty juice cup before returning to their seat."

"It is important that this be done with reverence," he told us. "I know it is a little different than we're used to, but to the Methodists it is an observance with roots as far back as their childhood faith. Tom, I want you to leave plenty of room between us to let each congregant experience a moment of reflection. And Clyde, don't come along too close behind Tom because I want each person to feel the love of Christ and to be fully aware of what they are doing." We nodded our understanding.

Clyde and I came in out of the rain that morning and sat in our pews. When the organist struck up the communion music we went to the front where Rev. Andrews handed us our trays, turned to the congregation and said, "Come, for all is ready."

The ushers invited people to move to the front one pew at a time. We had served about four pews of worshippers when I found myself looking down into the face of a little old lady. She reached for a cup of juice and I heard myself tell her, "This is Clyde's blood shed for you." ....OMG!

Fearing to meet her eyes, I gazed over her head at those four pews that I had already served wondering to how many of those worshippers I had offered Clyde's blood.

The rest of that service was just a blur to me. And it was three or four months before I worked up the courage to ask Reverend Andrews, "Did anybody complain about any irreverence at that Methodist communion?"

David said, "No, nobody said a word to me." Which is some indication of how much attention Methodists pay to the things you do for them. It was years before I worked up the courage to ask Clyde Dunlap if he heard me offering his blood to people. He hadn't.

Reflecting on that morning in recent years I've forgiven my trespasses in the matter. It was Clyde who had created the beautiful cabinetry in our country church: the organ loft, the choir loft, the altar itself. Clyde had even made the very table from which we served communion that morning. Surely that man, working with a hammer and a saw, at one time or another, had shed his blood in that very church.

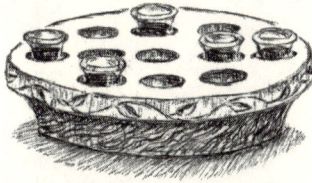

TOMMY

I am fond of asking others their earliest memory. To give them a minute to consider, I illustrate it with a memory of my own.

When I was four, maybe five years old we lived at number 45 half-way up Prendergast* Street in Jamestown, New York. Ours was a two-story yellow clapboard house on a single lot with a driveway covered with coal cinders shaken down in our hot air furnace. Oh! and a two-car garage out back that we never parked a car in. The other boys of the neighborhood lived near the foot of our hill not far from busy Washington Street. We each had our own collection of cars and trucks to play with so I was down there more than I was at home to play Cars and Trucks. "Cars and Trucks" was not a game with points and winners and

*See Author's Preface

losers. It was a term to describe what we were going to play or had been playing. First we settled on which of our lawns would be violated by construction that day. We needed dirt so, lacking a sand box, part of a lawn must be dug up, i.e. "excavated."

This memorable day the lawn we settled on belonged to Jack Lingenfelter. While turning a corner of Jack's front yard from a jungle to a construction site (grass to dirt) we added the essential ingredient for realism: sound! Boys are born with vocal chords designed to recreate the roar of an engine, the hesitation of the gear shift, and the rumble of acceleration. It's in the genes. *Vroom vroom, ahrum,* (gears shifting into fourth) *ahhhuuummm.* Drivers of dump trucks maneuvered under a handful of dirt and drove off to their destination where the truck bed lifted with hydraulic ease — *ummmm* and the dirt slid off where needed. All those muscular notes of truck driving — that's where men get their deep voices.

We were hard at work that summer's afternoon around supper time when my mother came out onto the porch of our house halfway up the block. She leaned out against the railing, looked down the street and called: "Tomm-ee."*

I was busy driving a truck. *"Remmm, ahruum ahhhuuummm."* I turned my head in her general direction and called back, "Coming." Then back to work:

*See Acknowledgements

remmm, vroom, ahrum, ahrum without looking up. I went right on playing.

Four, five minutes later my mother came back out on the porch, leaned over the railing to call: "Tomm-ee!"

"*Remmm, vroom, ahrum,* Coming! *ahrumm*" I didn't go that time either.

Minutes went by. Mother returned to the porch. This time there was a special timbre to her voice. Yelling, one might call it — "TOMM-EE!"

Vroom, ahrum ahhuuummm. "COMM-EENG!" *uummm, ahrum.* I didn't go that time either. I didn't go home until all my friends had been called in for supper by their mothers and there was nobody left for me to play with. So I strolled up the street until I was opposite my house. I crossed the brick street, stepping on the manhole cover for luck, up the stairs and onto the grass rug that covered our porch floor.

I pulled open the screen door and was surprised to find that the inside door was shut — the big wooden door to the house. This was a warm summer's evening and I didn't know why that door was shut. I reached for the handle on the big door. I turned it this way to find it stuck — then the other way — it was still stuck. So I called out, "Momm-ee."

From somewhere deep in the house came a voice: "Comm-ing!"

But she didn't come — I called again: "Momm-mee."

Once more from back in the gizzard of that house came a call: "Comm-ing."

She didn't come that time either.

With growing impatience I kicked the door with my foot and shouted "MOMM-EE!" At that moment I heard a sound from inside the door. A sound from up around the door knob — where the lock is… a rasping, metallic click. I thought to myself, this door isn't stuck — this door is locked!

The door opened no more than five, six inches wide. I could see the center part of my mother's face looking down. In those days I could get through a space five or six inches wide. I started through the doorway, but — a knee blocked the way. I looked up past the apron — to my mother's unsmiling face. "Yes," she said, "what do you want?"

I said, "I want to come in."

She said, "Who are you?"

What… what kind of a question was that, of your own little boy? Who am I!? I began to wonder. "I'm Tommy," I said. My lower lip quivered. Tears brimmed my eyes.

My mother said: "No, I don't think so."

"Yes!, I am. I'm your little boy," I sobbed.

"What did you say your name is?"

"My name (sob) is (sob) Tommy."

"Isn't that remarkable," she said. "I do have a boy named Tommy, but I don't think you're him."

"Yes! I am, I am him!"

"No… no, I don't think so. My Tommy, when I call him, he always comes. Now," she said, "you'll have to excuse me. We're having supper and I can't let strangers in the house." And she shut the door.

I stood out there tears ran down my dirty face, snot ran out my nose, my lower lip trembled. I cried my way across the grass rug. The porch railing came up to about my chin as I looked up and down the street where there was no one to comfort me, not even a dog. I looked down the street where all my little friends were safely inside their houses with their (sob) mothers who knew (sob) who they were. Behind me I heard the door open. I turned and there — praise God! — stood my own true mother right in the middle of the big, open door. She said, "Do you want to come in now?"

"Yes I do."

"All right," she said, pointing to the interior of the house, "you get in here. Wash your hands and wash that face and get up to the table."

Now, I'm here to tell you that nobody in our house ever forgot that night. My father didn't forget it to the day he died. My sister Miriam, the oldest, she didn't forget it till the day she died. My mother, she remembered it to the day she died. And my sister Jeanne, the middle child, she's never forgotten it. Jeanne told me in recent years, "I thought that night that I was never going to see my baby brother again. I couldn't even eat my supper."

And it was Jeanne who asked our mother just before she died, "Do you remember the night you locked Tommy out?"

"Yes, I do," said mother.

Jeanne said, "Didn't you feel terrible about that? That was just — it seemed so heartless, so tough. To say to a little boy no more than four or five years old that you weren't his mother and that this wasn't his house. That was terrible, you could have marked that boy for life."

Mother looked up from her sick bed. "That may all well be true," she said, "but I'll tell you this: from that day on, when I called that boy... he came."

MISTER FURLONG

There was a house of mystery on our street almost across from my house. The bungalow was cloaked in dark brown shingles, its hunched one-and-a-half stories brooded over the sidewalk. When we played kick-the-can in the brick street the house peered over our shoulders. We never ventured near the Furlong house, with the exception of Junior Churchill. As their paper boy he collected Journal money there every week.

It was a neighborhood understanding that Mr. Furlong was a peeping Tom. "Old Mr. Furlong," Junior alerted us, "spies on everyone without ever leaving his house. He bought a special, custom-made, peeping-Tom chair that spins around in a circle so he could look out of any window in his house through a pair of high-powered binoculars."

We never saw him leave the house. Maybe he slunk out at night to sneak around our windows after we were in bed, but he never came out in daylight.

Missus did. She kept rabbits in her backyard. She'd come out to clean the pen and feed her rabbits. She was as scary as her old man was. Every once in a while she'd come out and lie down on the grassy bank between her house and the house up the hill from her. She'd lie down on that grassy bank on her belly to sweep her hands back and forth combing the grass with her fingers.

Between the two of them, we decided the Furlong house was not a place we wanted to explore close up. We didn't go to the Furlong house even for Halloween. We figured the Furlongs would scare us more than we could scare them. Junior told us what it was like inside that house.

"It's dark," he said, "so dark they have lamps lit in the living room all day long. The lamp shades have tassels all around the bottom of 'em. And there's pillows. Lots of pillows — on the davenport, in the chairs, on the floor — everywhere, pillows. And rugs. Those people put rugs down on top of other rugs. Then, in the middle of the living room stands — *The Chair*.

It doesn't have legs. It sits on a stand bolted right into the floor. It can swivel around in any position he wants. He can look out the front windows, he can look down the hill, he can look up the hill, he can even look out into his backyard by looking through the windows in the dining room. That chair," he told us, "has a silver handle on the side.

When he pushes that handle down the chair goes down with him." Junior demonstrated by bending his knees to lower his body. "He pulls the handle up and the chair goes up with him. That's in case your bedroom window is higher or lower than he planned on. And," he added, "if you're not right at the window of your bedroom there's a little footrest on the chair so he can sit there with his feet up waiting for some girl to stand in front of her window… in her underwear.

"And binoculars," he said. "Right next to that chair there's a little round table holding a pair of big binoculars. Alongside the binoculars is a notebook. He writes in that notebook every day what girls he's seen and what color underwear they had on."

We got so we could tell when Old Man Furlong was watching us because we could feel it through our shirts. We would be out playing kick-the-can in the street of a summer's afternoon when one of us would stop and say, "Whew, boy am I hot." And they'd look at somebody and say, "Are you hot?"

And that person would say, "Oh, yeah, boy am I hot!"

And then everybody would say, "Yeah, I'm hot, too. Suddenly I'm just so hot." And then…

We would all turn our gaze at the Furlong house because it was a scientific fact that peeping Toms have hot eyes. And when that gaze from those hot eyes went through the binocular lens, it got magnified. It came out and landed on your body someplace, what he was looking at, and you would feel hot.

Now, it must have been easier to look out of the Furlong house than it was to look in. When we'd look over there what we would see is not tall maples like in front of houses on the rest of the street. No, there were two short trees growing with berries on 'em most of the year. And beyond the trees, the top of the porch came way out like a deep eyebrow shading the windows behind.

One Saturday morning my mother baked two cakes instead of the regular one. She baked a white cake with chocolate frosting for us and she baked a lemon cake with orange frosting. When that lemon cake had cooled my mother called me into the kitchen.

"I want you take this over to Mrs. Furlong," she said.

Take a cake to Mrs. Furlong! Doesn't she know? Hasn't anybody told the grown ups on this street about the Furlongs? "I don't want to go to the Furlong house!" I protested. "Why do I have to take a cake over there?"

"Because," she said, "Mrs. Furlong will be having people drop in on her for the next few days and she'll want to offer them something."

"How come? How come people are going there of all places? Nobody goes there except Junior Churchill to get his route money."

"Because last night Mr. Furlong passed away. He'd been sick for a long time," she said. "And it finally just carried him off."

I slid the cake tin and the cake off the table. What a gyp, I thought, we never get lemon cake with orange frosting and now this is going to the Furlongs. What a waste.

I crossed the street, stepping on the manhole cover for luck. There was already a car in the Furlong driveway parked next to that grassy bank where Mrs. Furlong sometimes came out and lay down. When I reached the front door on the porch I realized I was going to have to push the doorbell. That was something I was unwilling to do. Mr. Furlong's dirty finger must have pressed that doorbell more than once. So, I turned that cake pan enough to center the corner up against the doorbell. I leaned into it and rang the doorbell.

A tall, skinny woman I had never seen before opened the door.

"Well," she said, "what have we here?"

I held up the lemon cake with orange frosting.

"Come in," she said.

"Oh, no… no," I said. "No, this is for Mrs. Furlong."

"Yes, I know," she said, "but you should come in and present it yourself."

Then, before I knew it, she had her hand on my back and was guiding me into the dim interior of the Furlong house. As Mrs. Furlong made her way down the stairway from the upper level I stole a glance into the chamber of horrors and, — oh, my God! — there it was. Just like Junior described it: *The Chair*. And on a table right next to it was a pair of binoculars big enough to see clear over into bedrooms on Crossman Street, for sure.

I toyed with the idea of putting the lemon cake with orange frosting down on the Oriental rug and running, but I was too late. Mrs. Furlong stepped off the last stair and onto the rugs. She looked at me through red, moist eyes.

"Hello, Tommy," she said.

She knew my name!

"Nice of you to come over," she said.

I held up the cake tin, "This is for you from my mother."

She took it and said, "Oh my, doesn't that look delicious? You thank your mother for me."

The tall, skinny lady took the cake into the kitchen. Mrs. Furlong stepped toward the living room saying, "Would you like to come in and sit down a moment?"

I weighed my chances of getting a piece of my mother's lemon cake with orange frosting and I thought so far it hadn't been too terrible in the Furlong house. It was dark, yes, but I could see that the lamps with those tassels all around the shades were lit. And if Mrs. Furlong would just stay upright and wouldn't fall on the rug and start running her hand over it then maybe I would be safe.

I followed her into a room full of pillows and rugs and overstuffed furniture. My foot was no sooner over the threshold of that room when she motioned to *The Chair* and said, "Would you like to sit in Mr. Furlong's chair?"

Oh, jeeze! Oh, no! For only the second time in my boyhood I peed my pants. In haste, I said, "No! No thank you very much."

She stepped deeper into the parlor. "Mr. Furlong told me," she said, "if we had grandchildren, he would let them play in his chair." She stepped behind *The Chair* to run her fingers lovingly over the leather back, down the white porcelain arm and over the black leather armrest. "He loved to sit in this chair," she said. "He sat here for hours. He brought this chair with him when his illness forced him to close the barbershop. The chair reminded him of the years when he was healthy, happy and had company all day."

She moved to the front window to look out over the brick street and the houses across the way — one of which was mine. "I think men," she said, "have a hard time visiting other men who have gotten sick." After a moment she added, "He sat in that chair for hours, waiting for you children to come home from school." That made the hairs stand up on the back of my neck.

She turned to me then. "He always hoped you'd play in the street and wouldn't go up to the field where he couldn't follow your games. I think he always enjoyed your company."

She crossed the rugs to return to *The Chair*. "Have you ever looked through binoculars?" she asked.

I shook my head no.

"Well here," she said, "look through these." She lay them in my hands; they were heavy. "If it's not clear to you," she said, "turn this little dial on top until it becomes clear. Look out the front window. Maybe you'll see a bird out there." It took all my concentration to hold up the binoculars.

"We had those trees put out there to attract birds," she said. "He loved to watch birds. He collected birds like some people collect stamps." She motioned to the table. "In this notebook he wrote down every day what birds he'd seen."

It was a struggle just to hold the binoculars up. I don't think I ever did get them so everything was clear because I was listening to her talk about a man that I didn't know. None of us knew — all up and down Prendergast Street. I managed a "thank you" as I handed the binoculars back and started edging toward the door.

She followed me, laying her hand lightly on my shoulder. "Now that you've come once, maybe you'll come again."

I didn't say anything. I made my way to the door waiting for her to open it. She opened it and I stepped out onto the porch. From behind the screen door she said, "Maybe you can come back sometime to help me find sweet clover for my rabbits. Between my arthritis and my failing eyes, I have to get right down on the ground to find sweet clover."

When I heard her say that I turned around to look up at her. "I will," I said. "I will come back." Then I turned and walked down the steps trying not to walk like a boy with cold, wet underwear.

As I crossed the brick street toward my house I got to wondering who all had been playing kick-the-can that summer. Let's see, there would be Jack Lingenfelter, Jeep Golden, and Junior Churchill, Margaret Abbott, Mary Olson, and me.

I pictured us all standing there on the Furlong porch in a semi-circle around her door. There would be a princess and a cowboy and a pirate and a hobo, maybe Buck Rogers adjusting our false faces, getting ready to call out "Trick or Treat!" right after I pressed my finger on the doorbell.

DO YOU LOVE ME, MARY OLSON?

I finally stopped wetting the bed at 12-years-old just as I was awakening to the terrors of sex. If it wasn't one thing, it was another. Never a dry moment.

We boys of Prendergast* Street were maybe 12 or 13 years old. Some nights after supper we gathered at Luzzio's Grocery Store on the corner of Prendergast and Washington Streets. Washington Street was busy U.S. Route 17, a national artery linking the mills of the Midwest to the docks of New York. Across the way slender Italian men tended their truck farms in the black bottom land of the Chadakoin River.

We sat on the concrete steps in front of the store drinking from tall bottles of Nehi Orange pop. We drank the Nehi Orange to put out the fires in our bellies that came from eating whole sticks of Mr. Luzzio's

*See Author's Preface

59

homemade pepperoni. Every night: a stick of pepperoni and a Nehi Orange, with mosquitoes buzzing in our ears.

There was Jack Lingenfelter. Jack was six days younger and about fifty pounds heavier than I was all during our childhood, a big boy. There was Junior Churchill. Junior's mother made the best bread and rolls. We would spend Saturday mornings on Junior's back stoop. His mother came out with a roll for each of us, a pat of butter in the middle and hand them to us. And Eugene Golden; we called him Jeep after a character in the comics. Jeep was a fellow who never in his boyhood hit a baseball that didn't go through somebody's window.

There's two things boys talk about when they sit on steps like that. One is cars and trucks. The other isn't.

We talked a lot about Mary Olson. Mary Olson fascinated us. At that time in my life I had a natural fear of girls that left me chronically shy. The other guys, they wanted to make themselves known to Mary. They carried her books. They ran errands for her mother. One reason for it was Mary was about two, three years older than we were and was developing in ways that were very interesting to us. Also, Mary was new on our street, so she wasn't somebody you'd been wrestling with and playing kick the can with all your life. She was new and fresh and had this young, developing body.

I lived next door to Mary. Her house was the next one up the street from mine and our attic windows paired off across our cinder driveway. I didn't hang around Mary like the other guys. The same young body that stirred their inners scared me. I took only one action with respect to Mary Olson. I went up to my attic window which faced her attic window across the driveway. I printed out a sign. It said, quite simply: I LOVE YOU. DO YOU LOVE ME? I taped that sign in the window for Mary Olson to see sometime. Everything else I left up to her, half in hope, half in fear.

This one night down at the store I decided that I wanted to make myself a hero of Prendergast Street — I wanted to be thought of as the 'man' of Prendergast Street, even if I was only twelve. So what I did was I told those boys that Mary Olson had made what we used to call "advances" to me. That was a lie, but I tell you it got their attention.

They were all eyes and ears. "What!?" they gasped. "What did she do with you?" I described my attic in great detail, how you go up that set of stairs out my bedroom, and there's a little landing and some more steps to your right to go into the main part of the attic. "Well," I said, "I was just sitting there on the steps, you know, looking at the window not thinking much about anything, just watching cluster flies get caught in the cobwebs." I did not tell them about the sign; I thought that was something they didn't need to know. So I said, "I was sitting there and the next thing I knew I became aware of Mary Olson across the way in her attic window. She motioned to me to stay right where I was, and I did. And," I said, "Mary Olson started to unbutton her blouse."

Six eyes opened as wide as Skippy Cup lids. "She unbuttoned her blouse and she took it right off." Those boys looked at each other and smiled like old men. "And," I added, "I saw her in her brassiere." There was a great intake of breath. "Then," I said "she reached around and she unbuttoned her brassiere." There it was again. The B-word! At that point their eyes glazed over. They were cursing their fathers for having bought houses so far away from Mary Olson's.

Warming to the performance it occurred to me to introduce suspense. "She stepped up close to the window," I told them "and took her brassiere (pause) and she (pause) and she took it off (pause) and I saw (pause) her bosoms."

They gasped, leaning back against those concrete steps, unmindful that it was biting through their thin summer shirts. "Ohhh, Jesus," said Junior, with misplaced reverence. "What did she look like?"

It was the killer question.

What did she look like? I didn't know what Mary Olson looked like because I had never seen her bosoms. I had never seen anyone's bosoms. I was counting on them knowing what bosoms looked like. I had to say something. In the nick of time it became perfectly clear. There was something more I knew about chests.

So I leaned forward with what I imagined was a conspiratorial air and I said confidently, "She has hair on her chest."

"Hair?" said Jack.

"Hair!" said Jeep.

I could tell at once I had over-extended myself. I had gone beyond my understanding and I wallowed in ignorance. Those boys, who just moments before had been like cluster flies in the cobweb of my story were now all flying away, probably never to be caught by me again.

But something happened to me that night. Something in my loins happened. Oh, it wasn't because of Mary Olson. It was when I saw their eyes looking at me while I was telling them about Mary Olson. I realized what I most wanted to do in life was to tell stories.

That night as Mr. Luzzio pulled down the long shade behind his glass door and clicked off the neon sign and the sun sank over the celery fields as I walked home I made a vow to myself that if I was going to go on telling stories I had to work on the endings more.

Even today here in Vermont when I hear cluster flies gather at the windows of our warm spring and summer days I am transported back to Prendergast Street, up to number 45, up those attic stairs to that landing where I see in my mind's eye I am sitting, looking across the cinder driveway into Mary Olson's attic, past the tattered lace curtain wondering whether Mary Olson might yet come to her window to read my sign.

COUNTRY BOY

Here in Vermont, where I have lived the most of my life, residents of small towns are thought of as country people by those who live in our few cities. The valley town I live in has 2,400 souls, so to people in Burlington we're considered country people.

I grew up in Jamestown, New York, where a country boy or country girl was anybody from the farms and small outlying towns like Busti, Sinclairville, or Frewsburg. As a teenager I walked with my friends downtown on Friday nights to stand on the corner of Third and Main street to watch country folks pass by as they did their weekly shopping at the FW Woolworth and the Rexall Drugstore.

I had two older sisters for whom Friday nights downtown held no fascination. I was the third and last child that my mother bore. Mother never stopped referring to me as her 'baby' even into my forties. When I returned home she showed me off to her friends, put her arm around me and said, "This is my baby." Not one of those women ever batted an eye at that, having 40-year-old babies of their own.

The summer after I graduated from Syracuse University I worked on a track gang for the Erie Railroad, replacing worn-out ties and straightening rails. When I joined them the crew was made up of country boys.

That summer I struggled to be half as strong and half as smart about working as all those country boys who had been working hard since grammar school. It was hot, exhausting work; I came home wrung out at the end of each day.

In August when I was probably at my physical best my father was at his physical worst. He suffered two strokes close to each other. He could not talk so we could understand him and he had a hard time walking.

Late one afternoon my dad was getting some fresh air out on the porch shaded by the maples that cooled our street. I passed by the porch door and looked out to find my father lying where he had fallen, face up on the grass rug in front of the glider. His eyes were open and looking right at the doorway as if waiting for one of us to come by.

I called to my mother and went out on the porch. His pants were wet at the crotch where he had lost control of himself. This was a fastidious man; he shaved every day of his life. My father looked up at me, his eyes fixed on mine as if to say, 'I'm sorry you have to see me this way."

I lifted him off the grass rug in much the same way a country boy might pick up a sick calf. I cradled him in my arms and carried him upstairs like a doll. His eyes never left my own.

Those stairs — I remember him carrying me up, half asleep, to my bed.

He grew weaker over the next several days. Our family gathered in his room to tell stories of our growing up in that house.

The day before he died he grew animated, working hard to speak, to move his hands, to tell us something. After he died there in his bed, we three children sat downstairs in the breakfast nook trying to guess what he had wanted to say.

"It was probably that he wanted us to take care of our mother," I said. "So yesterday I assured him that she will be all right; the three of us will look after her."

Miriam, the oldest, disagreed. "I think he was asking for a cigarette." She was the only one of us who smoked. "He's smoked since he was 14," she said, "you don't know what it's like to go without a smoke."

We turned to look at our sister Jeanne, the middle child, waiting for her to choose between us. She looked down at her hands. Finally she said, "I think most likely he was telling us he loved us. He wanted us to know that before he died."

None of us ever knew for sure, but we learned something about ourselves the day we tried to figure it out.

My mother spent the following months meeting with attorneys and sorting out my father's possessions. She gave me a rain jacket of his, a necktie I had admired, his Masonic ring, and an old cardboard suitcase of his. I still wear his ring. I stayed at home helping mother through the fall. On December 30th I withdrew my boyhood savings from the Chautauqua County Bank.

I walked over to the Erie Depot and bought a ticket to New York City. That afternoon I walked down our street to say goodbye to Mr. and Mrs. Lingenfelter. I had a farewell cup of cocoa with old Mrs. Furlong, got my father's suitcase out of the attic, pausing on the landing to gaze across the driveway into the darkness of the Olson attic.

The next morning I laid my suitcase in the trunk of the family car and slid into the front seat next to Miriam who drove me down to the depot on Second Street.

And then I was on the train, riding my own rails through the small country towns. Away from Chautauqua County to New York City. Outside the Manhattan terminal, surrounded by the chaos of big city traffic, I waited for the light to change, then I crossed the street stepping on the manhole cover for luck. City people glanced from me to my cardboard suitcase, recognizing me for what I had been all along — a country boy.

ESTHER

On the night of August 24, 1963 in the upstairs bedroom of a bungalow in Jordans Crossing, Vermont, Otis Secoy jerked his head away from the pillow. "Did you hear that?"

"Yes," his wife Althea mumbled, "It's a train." They had been asleep maybe half an hour.

"Not damned likely!" he said. He swung his legs off the bed. The bulk of his 56-year-old body had earned him the nickname Bear. It tipped the mattress like a life raft. "Hasn't been a train through here for years. Those tracks are in no condition! Hell, I don't know if the bridge would hold a train! Still…" He sat on the edge of the bed, his ear cocked, his head motionless except for the eyes moving in concentration. Althea leaned on her elbow in the bedding behind him, her hand resting on the breadth of his back as if to draw courage from it.

"Maybe it was a coyote," she whispered.

"Shhh! If it was a train, that signal would have been for Roaring Branch Road. Listen." He didn't move on the bed for fear a creak from the old springs could mask the sound of a distant whistle.

There it was again! A locomotive howling a warning as it bore down on a grade crossing.

"By Jesus, it is a train!" He leaped from the bed, rushed to the window and rolled up the shade. "Can't believe it. Comin' from the north." He strained to see through the fog that had crept up from the river as they slept, cloaking the lumber sheds across the tracks. He called over his shoulder, "What the hell time is it, anyway?"

Althea reached for the alarm clock. "Little after eleven," she said.

Bear pressed his forehead against the window pane. Their house was on Short Street where the tracks intersected the lumberyard. He knew if it was a train, about now it would be rumbling over the trestle spanning Roaring Branch. Once past the sugarhouse it would reach the curve that opened onto the lumber yard. Bear already saw the fog to his left slowly glow yellow as it picked up the headlight of the oncoming train.

"There's the light of it," he called. "Come see!" Althea swung her legs over her side of the bed to find her slippers on the braided rug, but by now he was moving toward the doorway. "Let's go down to the porch," he called. "I can't believe this!"

They scrambled down the stairway and out onto the porch. There, growing brighter with each turn of the great drive wheels, the locomotive headlight was taking shape in the fog as steam wailed through the whistle. The porch shook. The squeal and clanking of the flanges grinding against the curving tracks filled the night air. The howl of the steam whistle echoed back from the lumber sheds as the train rumbled toward the Short Street crossing.

Bear stood transfixed, his thigh resting against the porch railing, Althea at his side. Her fist knotted the back of his undershirt. "What is it?" she asked. "Where is it coming from?" As the hulking locomotive roared nearer, its illuminated number plate came into view. 1445.

"The old night train from Rutland," Bear said. "I'll be damned!" He took a step backward to the safety of the shadows afforded by the porch ceiling. "I'll be goddamned!"

The locomotive rumbled past Short Street from where, by the glow of the firebox inside, they saw the outline of the engineer leaning from the cab window, his eyes scanning the tracks ahead as the great machine rattled over the crossing. A coal tender and five other cars rocked after it toward the rusting steel skeleton that remained of a bridge.

"He'll never make it across!" Bear said. "That bridge won't hold him!"

But the locomotive clanked and groaned over the trestle and rolled around the curve on the far side, the train's passage marked by the receding sound of the wheels rolling across the rail joints.

Bear ventured barefooted onto the street and down to the tracks. He ran his finger over them to see if the train had rubbed any rust off. It hadn't. He peered at the grade crossing.

His mind went back to that September night thirty years before, a night he had been living with every day since. Spread over two or three yards down the middle of the tracks, he and Althea had come upon the mangled body of a small child in a bloodied white nightdress.

Some time later and 1100 miles distant in a small town in Iowa, the Abramson family of three gathered over breakfast.

"Did you read the story in *Grit* about Jordans Crossing?" Paul asked between sips of coffee. He kept a sentimental subscription to the rural newspaper his grandparents had taken in his boyhood.

His wife Louise slid scrambled eggs from the pan onto three plates. "In Vermont? Your Jordans Crossing?"

"Yeah, about a ghost train supposedly coming through town in the middle of the night on abandoned railroad tracks."

"Here, Esther, let mommy sprinkle Cheerios on your tray — crunchy, yum! So, a train? What kind of train?"

"A train!" he said. "I don't know what kind. A freight I think it is. Says there are some locals who swear it came through town and others who just roll their eyes about it." He jiggled a ketchup bottle over his eggs.

She motioned with her hand. "You want that last piece of toast?" He slid the toast her way. "Mass hysteria," she said. "Be a lot of doctoral theses on that, you can bet." His face clouded over. "I'm sorry, Paul," she said. "This must bring back memories for you. It would for your mother."

"Well, that was before I was born. I was born in June, 1934. Esther had died the previous fall. Long time ago." He focused on their little girl across the table. "I've never known why things happened the way they did. I'm not sure my mother does either. Anyway, she doesn't talk about it."

Jordans Crossing had been the center of the so-called Jordan Job back in the days of clear cutting hard woods for the growing northeastern furniture industry. Paul's paternal grandfather, Michael Abramson, was an engineer on the railroad that brought logs and lumber over to Troy, New York. Paul's father, Mike Junior, had followed his father's tracks and settled in the hamlet that remained of Jordans Crossing. The family's modest white clapboard house on Short Street lay but a stone's throw from the passing trains.

Before Paul was born, a sister, Esther, had been hit and killed by a train near the family home. The story surrounding the event came down to him piecemeal through his childhood like an inheritance that was never quite paid in full. The little girl's remains were laid to rest on a knoll behind her grandparents' farmhouse in Iowa.

"Maybe there's a connection with the accident," Paul said. "Maybe it's a ghost." Their own little Esther was happily tossing Cheerios onto the linoleum. Leaning over to retrieve some, he added, "Could be the guy that hit my sister."

One September night when the first Esther was two years old she had wandered away from the house and onto the tracks. The night train came through and hit her. No more than a month later, his father had also been killed by a train.

On the rare occasion when she talked to Paul about their deaths, his mother, Grace, spoke of his sister without making eye contact as if in Paul's eyes she might see her little girl and grieve anew. He got short sentences from her about it as if she hoped for an interruption to distract them both.

No one in southern Vermont could recall when last a ghost had been the subject of an article in the warning for a special town meeting, but there it was on the agenda that Herm Benedict, Chair of the Board of Selectmen, read aloud to the assembly. "What do voters want the Selectmen to do about people who gather these nights up at Jordans lumber yard to watch for the so-called 'ghost train'? These gatherings disturb residents of Short Street."

Some thought the article was a joke. It wasn't. It was an attempt by Herm and other officials of Jordans

Crossing to rid themselves of midnight phone calls from irate citizens. Herm said to the Town Clerk that evening, "They've got to either tell us what they expect us to do about it or leave us be!"

Otis "Bear" Secoy had come to be the one most people looked to for information or, more likely, speculation about "the train." He and Althea lived hard by the main line train tracks in town where they had witnessed the first appearance of the phantom train. Herm asked him to sit up front with the Selectmen that night. Bear took off his visored Blue Seal feed cap and sat down.

Herm slid the microphone over to him. "Maybe you should bring folks up to speed on this," he said. "Half of 'em say nothing's there. That just makes the others mad."

Bear started in. "Back two years ago Althea and me were in bed together" — the wooden chairs creaked with laughter — "when this big old steam train came through town right across from where we live. Only it wasn't a train. Couldn't be a real train is what I'm sayin'. It looked like a train, sounded like a train, smelled like a train, but after it was gone there was no sign it was ever there. For one thing, the bridge over the river couldn't stand up to a locomotive passing over it, let alone one haulin' a coal tender, a couple tank cars, a box car or two, and a caboose. This thing came back three nights last year and two nights so far this year. Always toward the end of August."

He stopped there, uncertain where to take up the story next. The folding chairs were silent. Herm Benedict leaned over to Bear who covered the microphone with a calloused hand. "The railroad company," said Herm, "tell 'em about the railroad company."

Bear went on. "The railroad company, what's left of it, of course says there's been no train over those tracks for..." he rubbed the stubble on his cheek, "well, probably twenty years now. For a while they'd send a little track inspection car up and down once every summer. They don't even pay for that now." He leaned back to signal the end of his participation.

Herm pulled the microphone over to himself. "So that's pretty much what we know or don't know. What we're hoping for tonight is to find out what the voters propose we do about all the people congregating up there these nights disturbing the peace and leaving litter around the lumber yard for Mr. Jordan and his help to pick up in the morning." Without smiling he added, "Or just maybe you're the ones carrying on up there." Averted eyes, shifting feet, nervous laughter.

Bear pulled the mike back. He held up his left thumb. "First off, the railroad knows nothin' about any trains on the Rutland Bennington line." His left index finger joined his thumb. "Second of all, this train, or whatever it is, don't bother nobody but us. Nobody has seen hide or hair of it either north or south of the lumber yard." Third finger. "Whatever it is isn't leavin' any mark. The rails are as rusty the morning after as they were the night before." Fourth finger. "There's no schedule to its comin' except it only comes in late August or around there." Little finger. "Not everybody sees it. Even on Short Street there are folks who stand next to us when it comes through who can't see it."

Isabel Greene in the second row called out. "I say it's the ghost of the train killed that little girl up there."

Bear looked her way. "The Abramson child was killed back in '33. Why now, thirty years later, are we seeing this train? There's nothing to connect 'em. The dates don't even match. The little girl was hit, I think, in September that year." Murmured nods rippled through the chairs.

From the middle of the chairs a hand went up. Herm Benedict nodded in that direction and a man stood. It was Mr. Bishop. Locals referred to him as a newcomer though he and his family had for years been summer visitors. When met in the grocery he was deferred to most likely because his big city barbers had fashioned a classic Van Dyke on his chin.

"I have never heard Word One about an accident on that crossing," he said. "If there was a death, why wasn't a signal gate erected over there?"

Bear leaned into the mike again. "It was a child killed. No cars involved. No use for a gate. A child can just walk under a gate."

"And the child's parents? Where were they when it happened?" The hall drew in a breath. Bear glanced at the Select Board. Their eyes retreated to the papers on the table before them.

Bear softened his voice to say, "The little girl wandered away from home that night. Her mother was at home… asleep. The father… was at work."

Bishop persisted. "If not everyone can see this 'train', then who besides you and Mrs. Secoy can?"

"I'd have to let 'em say for themselves," Bear said. "It's come to the point where some people I'm sure have seen it now say they didn't because they don't want people thinkin' they're looney."

"Well," said Mr. Bishop, "can you tell us: men, women, townspeople, outsiders?"

"Men and women, both, but not all. Some do, some don't. No kids. Never knew a kid to see it. Most likely you've gotta have kids in order to see it. Don't ask me why."

"What difference could that make?" asked Bishop.

"Beats me. All I know is I see it. My wife sees it. Her sister Felicity from Bellows Falls don't. Even standing on our porch with us one night when it come through."

"And she doesn't have kids?"

"Felicity is a nun." Laughter filled the hall. "Also Pastor Greenwold from the Congo Church, he's seen it, though he won't always admit to it. Father Lorenz from St. Peter's can't... though he wants to in the worst way. It don't matter if you're a native or a flatlander. Don't matter if you're Catholic, Protestant, or Holy Roller. But more'n likely, if you've had a kid somewhere along the line, man or woman, you'll see it. If you *are* a kid, an old maid, a priest, a nun, or just too ugly to make babies with, chances are you're out of luck." Laughter from every row.

Bishop turned from Bear to the Selectmen at the table. "What kind of action do you want from us tonight?"

Herm Benedict slid his chair back to rise to his feet. "What I'd most like is not to get any more midnight phone calls complaining about people hangin' around the lumber yard. But I'm not keen on puttin' a curfew on just one section of town... probably not legal."

By 9:30, only the diehards remained, and they decided to table the mess. That was all the townspeople could agree to do with a phantom train whose engineer was hell-bent on running it 350 yards down rusty mainline tracks on foggy summer nights.

In June of 1943 Paul Abramson turned nine. His schoolmates made Father's Day greeting cards for their fathers, many of whom were in the service. Paul's father had died in a railroad accident before Paul was born. So he made his card for his grandfather with whom he and his mother had lived since his birth. At the dinner table that Sunday his mother told stories about growing up with her father. The old man quickly winked disclaimers. Paul glanced from one to the other around the table, smiling at their jibes, eye rolls and reminiscences until, still smiling and eager to share in the fun, he said, "What was my father like?"

His grandparents looked over at his mother who averted her eyes toward the casseroles on the lace cloth. The boy tried to assess the sudden silence by looking to each in turn, his gaze finally settling on his mother. She met his eyes. "Paulie," she said, "we'll talk about that this afternoon. You and I, okay?"

While Paul and his mother did dishes together she talked nonstop about the people at the school where she taught, whether his grandmother would attend Ladies Aid on Monday, pretty much anything that wasn't about Paul's father. His grandfather had taken up a defensive position at the kitchen table, armed with his crossword puzzle and a pocket dictionary. Finally his mother removed her apron and said to the room, "Paulie and I are going for a little walk."

She stepped off the back porch in the direction of the cow barn. "Let's go this way," she said. As if on cue, Specks, the gray-muzzled farm dog struggled to her feet to limp off after them. Along the way Paul bent to pull from the weeds a grass seed-head and stem which he clamped between his teeth. He imagined it made him look older, ready for adult talk.

They entered the barn's gaping doorway to be enveloped by the cool darkness within. Ahead of them on concrete blocks rested his grandfather's red 1929 Ford pickup with its spare tire rakishly mounted on the running board. To their left stretched three rows of unused stanchions garlanded with dusty cobwebs reaching to the rough-hewn floor.

Paul and his mother sat down side by side on two bales of hay. At their feet, in a square of sunlight falling from the cupola overhead, the old dog circled a bed for herself. Paul regarded his shoes while his mother prepared to force words from her parched throat. She spoke evenly in rehearsed tones.

"Paul, your father would have loved sitting around the table today, telling us stories about growing up in Vermont, and answering your questions about railroading. But you remember our telling you about the accident?" He admitted he did.

"When Esther died your father was terribly upset for weeks. We both were, of course, but in your father's case, he sank into a deep depression. That means that everything in someone's life becomes dark. Food doesn't taste good. A depressed person just wants to go to sleep and never wake up. Your father got this kind of sickness and it was wearing him out."

She said nothing for what seemed a long time to young Paul. She reached her hand out to stroke the dog's head as if to comfort. Or be comforted. The dog raised her head into the gesture.

"After Esther's death," she said, "Mike worked in the daytime. He was in bed early every night. At the sound of a whistle he turned his head away from the window and cried. He was out of his mind with grief. He felt guilty, as all parents do, when they fail to shield their children from harm. In the end that killed him. Your father died of a broken heart."

"But you told me a train hit him!"

"Yes, it did. Remember, his head was filled with memories of Esther. With the image of Esther's...", her gaze retreated to her folded hands, " ...terrible death. He couldn't think clearly. And that day, in the Bennington yards, he simply turned left when he should have turned right. A small mistake, but it put him in front of a switch engine. And that's why your father isn't here to tell you his stories."

She told herself that she had answered his question. She had done what he asked of her.

They sat on the bales in silence until she stood and moved to the doorway with Paul following. The dog lifted herself with effort and plodded in their wake.

In his teens Paul's feelings for his absent father deepened. He struggled with his sense of loyalty and his feelings of abandonment. His search for justice fell just short of his grasp. He bristled at perceived judgments offered by his grandmother when talking about Mike. Her digs, with which he had grown up, no longer went over a little boy's head. More than once she had mumbled about "the moral cowardice of men."

"What is that supposed to mean?" he challenged her.

"Never you mind," she said in her practiced adult-to-child voice.

One afternoon in the car Paul asked his mother, "How come you had my sister's body actually dug up in Vermont and brought here to be buried all over again?"

"Grandma paid for that. If she couldn't bring both of them to Iowa it was important to bring her grandchild. Mike was tough enough to remain where he was. He was a Vermonter."

"It's unfair to leave someone outside family like that. Like he had the Black Plague, for Pete's sake! It was mean." Looking at the road ahead, he added, "When I die I want to be buried next to my father!"

She glanced at him without responding. A mile or two went by and he spoke again.

"If it was just money you could have used the money you got from the railroad. Wasn't there insurance for their engineers? He died on the job, didn't he?"

"Yes, he was at work, but there was no settlement. Company lawyers made the case that his accident was the fault of his own carelessness."

"He killed himself? That's what they thought?"

She licked her dry lips.

"What did your lawyer say?"

She pulled the car to the shoulder of the road, left the motor running and turned to face him.

"Paul, I had no money for a lawyer. We spent what small savings we had to bury our little girl. There wasn't even money to bury your father. The crewmen from Rutland came down. They hammered together a coffin. They dug a grave in the cemetery and we put him in there. They passed the hat up and down the line until they got enough for a headstone. But that was after I'd gone."

"So you've never seen the grave marker?"

"No, but I have a picture of it. Somewhere in grandpa's desk."

"What made you leave Vermont?"

"Money. Winter was coming on. I had house payments. Mike's income was gone. I had no training for factory work. Even so, it was 1933; there weren't jobs anywhere, especially for a pregnant widow lady. At least here in Iowa Grandma and Grandpa had that big garden back of the house, the orchard, and all the milk you could drink."

When they got home that day he stood by the desk until she handed him the snapshot. A simple headstone said "Michael P. Abramson." A second line read, "The Professor." Then came his dates. At the bottom was the image of a steam locomotive in more detail than Paul thought possible on such a small stone.

"What's this about a professor?"

"Mike wore glasses, round with steel rims to take rough handling. The guys thought they made him look like a professor. It was his nickname at work."

"Can I have this picture?"

"Don't lose it."

In his room he secured one edge of the photo between the glass and the frame on the mirror where he could see it whenever he wanted.

On a September afternoon in 1953 Paul sat at the dining room table puzzling over his first homework of the year. Earlier that day he had overheard his grandfather say that it was the anniversary of Esther's "passing," making it sound as if his dead sister had moved up a grade in school. On impulse Paul slid his chair back and strolled into the parlor where his grandfather sat next to the floor lamp reading *Country Gentleman* magazine. Paul plopped himself into the rocker on the other side of the lamp. His mother, snuggled into the corner of the davenport opposite, was darning socks on a wooden egg.

Paul spoke to his mother. "Tell me more about the accident."

Her expression didn't change. She continued to close the hole in the sock. "There's nothing more to tell," she said.

"Jeez, Mom! How'd she get out of the house? How come the engineer didn't stop? Did they fire him? Did Dad want to kill him?"

Grace wove the thread with deliberation, hoping an answer would come to her, one that said little so she could face her reflection in the kitchen window tomorrow. But the silence worked against her. She heard the soft crumple of her father's magazine being lowered to his lap. Her mother stood listening by the kitchen door. Grace appealed to God for help before remembering that God had died the same night Esther had.

She lowered her hands, still holding the egg and her needle, giving her something to look at in her lap.

"Your sister was only two," she said, her voice barely audible. "But she had the skills of an acrobat when she put her mind to something. She climbed out of her crib somehow." She glanced at Paul's grandfather. "I've searched my mind for an answer, but I can't give you one. She would have made her way downstairs. It was easy for her," she allowed herself a passing smile of remembrance, "just turn around and slide step to step on her tummy. The porch door was right off the foot of the stairs."

"Where were you?"

"In the kitchen."

"Doing?"

"Canning apples."

She waited. There was no follow-up question.

Paul's eyes scanned the parlor, registering nothing as his mind erected a screen against which he now could project the scene she was describing.

"I canned sliced apples or applesauce most every night when Mike was at work and Esther had gone to bed. Times were hard. Mike sold them to the men for their lunch boxes."

"Yeah, okay, go back to Esther."

"Esther must have wandered off the porch and into the yard." Although ever so slowly, Grace herself was wandering where she had not intended to go.

"Once in the yard she had a choice between turning up the street toward the dead-end or down the slope toward the grade crossing. Apparently she chose the easier course and toddled down."

Paul grimaced at the innocence of the word. Grace observed that and hoped it might have distracted his attention. It didn't.

"She got as far as the main tracks where, for some reason, she turned off the street and stepped between the rails. The stones must have hurt her bare feet." She probed her apron pocket for a handkerchief.

"Trying to get away from the stones, a foot must have slipped under a rail and got caught there."

For a moment neither said anything. Paul had followed it all in his mind's eye. "Weren't they looking ahead? They were going through a town, forgodsake!"

An inexperienced interrogator, Paul was unaware that he had backed his mother into a corner, a danger to them both. Grace's knuckles whitened around the darning egg, but no amount of counter pressure could control what had gathered in her breast. What she had never truly seen rose again to fill a mother's head — the cruelly named "catcher" rolling unchecked toward the little body, the strident whistle mocking a baby's cries for her mother.

"Jesus!" she snapped. "It wasn't the engineer's fault, dammit." She hated him for not knowing what she had been keeping from him. "I am a bad mother. I told her a story I shouldn't have and it killed her!" she screamed. She threw the darning egg at him with the speed of a hardball. "There!" she sobbed. "You happy?"

Paul scrambled to his feet, shaking and crying. He was afraid for her. He'd never seen her face that ugly.

Her sobs threatened to drown her breath.

Paul's grandmother hurried to her daughter's side.

"I didn't know all this," Paul's words quavered with tears. "Why don't I know all this?"

"Because it's none of your business!" Grace shouted from the davenport.

Paul turned to his grandfather. "How is she a bad mother?" Stunned by the moment, his grandfather gave no answer.

His grandmother frowned at him from across the room. "Be still, Paul," she told him. "It's a family story your mother hates to tell and we hate to hear. We'd be happy if we never had to hear it again." She pulled her own weeping "little girl" closer. And added softly, to Grace alone, "Ever."

Later when Paul sat, unseeing, before his books in the dining room, his grandmother passed by on her way to the kitchen. She leaned into his neck to whisper, "Don't be looking under any more rocks, boy."

Before supper, near the horse trough, Paul sought out the biggest rock he could move. He upended it. A whole other world opened to the sunlight. Hundreds, no, thousands of creatures skittered in all directions, desperate to hide once more from the light of day.

Early the next morning Grace came to Paul's room where his head was still under the covers. She sat on the bed until he stirred and awoke. "Oh, Paulie, no words can say how ashamed I am. I am so terribly sorry. What I said hurt all of you last night, but especially you. I'm praying you will find it in your heart some day to forgive your mother… forgiveness comes painfully slow. I ask now that it will come to all of us in the family — to me, to you, and to your father, God rest his soul."

At that her son lifted his sleep-fogged head to look in her eyes.

"Why my father?"

"Because," she said, "for better or worse, when I needed him most he wasn't there."

The day of Paul's high school graduation his grandfather called from the parlor. "Paulie, come in here, your mother and I have something we want you to have." He crossed the room to the roll-top desk where the old man sat before an opened drawer. His mother rested her arm on the desktop. His grandfather reached into a bulky manila envelope and slid something out. "Here, Gracie, you should give him this." She closed her fingers around it. He then tilted the envelope, sliding the remaining contents out onto the green desk blotter — papers mostly, certificates, booklets, letters, envelopes and a curling photograph.

"These were your father's," the old man said. "Your mother hung on to them figuring that one day the time would seem right to pass them along." He moved his arthritic fingers among the papers, poking them apart.

"These are old timetables from Vermont. The town of Jordans Crossing is in there. Maybe his train is in there someplace."

Grace leaned toward him. "No, Dad," she said, "that's a passenger timetable. Mike ran a freight train."

"Here is a postcard of some passenger station or other along the line. Here's his engineer's certificate. Here's a letter of commendation from the president of the company for ten years of service."

He separated and smoothed out a posed photograph curling into itself. "This appears to be everyone who worked out of the Rutland terminal, all lined up." Grace intercepted the photo when he lifted it up toward Paul. She studied it before handing it over to Paul. "Can you find him in there?" she asked.

Paul took the photo. He saw workingmen wearing bib overalls and soft-visored caps favored by railroad men. They were posed at the front of a locomotive, leaning against it, and perched on every available space from the cowcatchers to just under the headlight stands. Most were unsmiling to remind the world that railroading is serious business. One man smiled out from behind round steel-rimmed eye-glasses. "Right there," he pointed.

Paul smiled back at the face under the number plate. He pointed to the tops of the locomotives. "What are those domes on top of the engines?"

His grandfather held the photograph close to his face. He pointed. "This one's a steam dome and the other's a sand box. Pull a lever inside the cab and sand trickles down through pipes out onto the rails. Gives you traction in snowy Vermont."

The old man looked up at his daughter, nodding his head in the direction of her son. Taking her cue, Grace opened her hand to reveal a large railroad pocket watch with its attached chain, its hinged cover engraved with the image of a steam engine and coal tender. She pressed the release. The cover sprang open revealing a simple watch face with Roman numerals. She held it out. "I've wound it," she said. "I can't get it to run, but it's worth your keeping for all that."

Cradling the time piece in his palm, Paul ran his fin-ger-tips over the metal. "It's not gold," said the old man. "You got gold when you retired. It's brass most likely. I'm guessing he got it with that 10-year commendation."

Paul's grandfather rose from his chair. "I'm going to let you two Abramsons look these over together." He gave Paul's shoulder a squeeze and left.

Grace straightened the papers on the desk blotter. "I want you to know, Paul," she said, "that you're a very special person… a gift… a gift from your father to me and a gift from me to your father. When Esther died, your father said he had let her down by not keeping her from harm. He lay in bed sleepless until the night train passed through town. When we heard the whistles we cradled each other and cried. One of those nights we held each other so close that your life began in our sorrow."

She cleared her throat to push aside a thickening that gathered there. "One day, not long after, the doctor told me that someone was growing inside of me." She reached for his hand. "That was you, Paul! I was so happy! I could hardly wait for your father to come home to tell him. That was the night your father didn't come home.

"It took about all the strength I had left to pack everything up, leave The Crossing and come back here. The very next June you were born here in Iowa. I think if your father had known you were on the way, Paul, he might not have died. You might have been his salvation."

Paul imagined those rough hands lifting him from the crib to hug him against a faded blue cotton work shirt, hands that might one day teach him how to drive a locomotive, stack wood, change a car's oil, stalk the white tail, and sing harmony.

That summer Paul said he wanted to visit his father's grave site, but when he asked about reviving the 1929 pickup, his grandfather allowed it was not likely to survive the trip there and back. More to the point, Paul would have to begin work the next day and work all summer to earn money for books.

Paul entered teachers' college at Iowa State where, in his third year, he met dark-eyed Louise, a girl from upstate New York who, over time, drew a curtain of romance over his thoughts about Vermont cemeteries. Louise was pretty in a girl-next-door Jane Wyman way: athletic, musical if you count the marching band (which he did), slender and two inches taller than he which mattered only on the dance floor. They were sweethearts before Thanksgiving break, spent with his family at his grandparents' house.

After many more weekend visits to the farm, Paul proposed on a cold moonlit January night at the foot of the campanile on campus. An occasion, she would later remind him, an English major would stage so that their grandchildren could return one day to stand in that place.

They were married on a blue-sky Saturday the summer of their graduation. That evening as they stood next to his grandparents' sedan, offered for a weekend honeymoon, Paul lifted a grain of rice from his bride's hair, opened his father's watch case and dropped it in.

The following August, prior to the birth of their first child, Paul told Louise, "If it's a boy, I'd like to name him after our two grandfathers."

"Let's see," she said. "Ellsworth and Bruce. Sure,"

She chuckled, "At least it'll please both families." They were quiet for a moment. not looking at each other. "And for a girl," she said, "…Esther."

He frowned. "Won't happen," he said. "Be too much. Too many memories for my mother. She'll say, 'That won't bring her back.'"

"She's right," said Louise, "it won't. But in a small way, in a different way, it has the potential. Names are important, Paul. We're remembering our grandfathers when we keep their names alive."

"Yeah, but to remember Esther is to remember the accident, something my mother wants to forget."

She leaned toward him, her hand on his knee. "How about if I ask her at the shower tomorrow?"

"Well, good luck with that!"

The next day, when the shower guests had gone, Louise and Grace relaxed over a cup of tea.

"We have chosen the name for a boy," Louise told her.

"You have?"

"Bruce Ellsworth."

"How thoughtful! My father will be pleased. And for a girl?"

Louise took a breath. "We're thinking about Esther."

Grace stiffened, shook her head. "I do wish he'd let go of all that!"

"Mother, it's my idea." Their eyes met. "Paul said you wouldn't like it."

Grace frowned. "Louise, I live through it in my heart every single day. You know how I feel."

"That it was somehow your fault."

Grace's hands tightened into fists. "It *was* my fault!"

"Even if that were true, and I don't believe it, we now have a chance to bring our baby into the family with a name any little girl could love. When you hear someone say 'Esther' you would be filled with joy once more. I wish you would say 'yes' to us. To me."

Louise's tender entreaties touched Grace in her guarded heart. Tears came in spite of her wishes. She sought to retreat into what was left of any safe place within. Weary of measuring her words, first with her son and now with this sweet girl, she surrendered to tears.

Louise knelt at her side. "Oh, Mom." She cradled her as best she could with gentle rocking, murmuring over and over a consoling tune that sprang unbidden from her own infancy, a wordless lullaby sung to her when she needed it.

In the morning Grace took Louise aside. "You are such a dear girl, Louise. You don't know how happy I am that you're in our family. I'm happy, too, that you will mother my grandchildren. Esther's a lovely name. And if we promise to let her be the Esther she is and not the Esther who was we'll honor both girls. So I say, go ahead, with my blessing. Esther is my grandmother's name. Now there was a *feisty* soul if there ever was one. About now she's jumping up and clicking her heels somewhere in heaven."

Those first weeks after Esther's birth would stay with Paul the rest of his life. Strange dreams disturbed his sleep, beginning, he would later recall, almost from the day Esther was born. His days were filled with the new baby. But his nights unleashed dreams of a world he'd not seen before, vivid, memorable — and filled with images of trains.

One night a locomotive maybe five times normal size steamed out of a forest to loom over him. He was helpless — afraid to stay — afraid to run. More than once he found himself trapped inside a train. Not a passenger car, but a featureless sort of car from which he couldn't escape. Through the side he could see townspeople milling about trackside. He called out to them. He banged on the wall, but couldn't make himself heard. An undefined sense of urgency swept over him.

How much, he wondered, does his grandfather know about what happened in Vermont? "Ask your mother about that," he would be told. Paul suspected his grandparents of protecting Grace — and through Grace — even him — but from what? And whom?

To celebrate Esther's first birthday, the family gathered at the old homestead to help Esther blow out the single candle on a cake. Esther's great-grandparents each held her for a round of snapshots. "That's about all the excitement this old man can take for one birthday," said Paul's grandfather. Paul helped him into the parlor for a lie-down on the davenport. He lay there alone, just inside the open windows overlooking the wide porch, bathed in the sweet music of family voices accompanied by the rustling oak leaves overhead.

It was Paul, come in to say goodbye, who found the body on the davenport. He knelt, enfolded his Grandfather in his arms, laid his cheek against his grandfather's cheek and wept. With the old man gone Paul was left in a family of women, something he worried might diminish his chances of learning the full story of Jordans Crossing. There was no doubt now. He would have to find a reason to return, for the first time, to The Crossing. He found the reason within a year.

In June of 1965 Louise flew east to spend ten days in Cooperstown, New York, with her ailing mother, to allow her sister, Jeanne, some respite time with her husband. Their mother died the night her sister returned home. After the funeral Louise lingered as long as she dared leave Paul with little Esther, then flew home.

Two months later, just prior to Esther's second birthday, Jeanne telephoned from Cooperstown. "I've been trying, with diminishing success," she told Louise, "to sort things out in this house. Could you come back for a few days to help me decide what to do with what's left of Mom's stuff so we can finally get the house on the market?"

"Yes, of course, but what about Esther? She'll demand a lot of attention out there. Let me ask Paul."

Paul jumped at the chance. "Let's all go!" he said. "We'll take turns driving." He laughed, "I'll take Esther to the Baseball Hall of Fame for her birthday! Better yet I'll take her over to Vermont for a day. Can't be more than three or four hours from your mother's."

"Looks like it's all set," Louise told Jeanne.

"I'll visit the grave," he told her, "take snapshots of the old house. The two of us will stay overnight somewhere. We'd be back by suppertime Thursday, Esther's birthday."

"Okay, as long as you'll keep track of her once you get back. I'm not all that thrilled about having a two-year-old underfoot. But promise you'll be gone for just one night! I want Esther back here for her birthday." It was agreed then. She packed their bags. She, Paul and Esther left the next morning.

The day after arriving in Cooperstown Louise put together a tote bag of Esther's travel necessities: Cheerios, Doll Baby, favorite blanket, diapers, bottles, toothbrush and nightdress. Paul and Esther left the closet cleaning, carton stuffing, and attic exploring to the two women and drove northeast, playing counting games along the way. "How many cows? How many red barns? How many doggies? How many children?"

Before he got into New York's capital district traffic he pulled into a rest stop for a diaper inspection and a snack. They shared a Run-Around session to ease growing evidence of two-year-old restlessness after too many miles in the back seat. It worked. She napped while he picked his way through heavy traffic around Albany and Troy. He found the roads less traveled that led eastward through the Taconics toward the Green Mountains. As they crossed the Vermont state line the highway narrowed and the hills closed about them. The two-lane road funneled them through a gap between hemlock-softened hills and the waters of a shallow river bed. The sky threatened a shower before the day was out.

He checked in at the rambling Colonial Inn, a hostelry of a certain age in need of cosmetics and a handy man. He was given a second-floor room with a double bed and a paint-chipped crib he had to move himself. With effort he could glimpse Main Street through the railing of the full-length second floor porch that had begun to lean toward the sidewalk below.

The desk clerk gave him directions to the cemetery on the edge of town. He drove slowly into the tree-shaded grounds, but with no idea where to start he soon set out to explore by foot. On the west side the land fell away abruptly, opening to an unobstructed view of the Taconic range. Along the foot of the embankment ran the abandoned tracks of the Rutland Railway.

At the top of the embankment he found his father's grave next to a shallow depression in the grass. He dropped Esther's hand to kneel by the marker. He brushed grass mowings from the stone.

"Here I am," he said.

With his fingertips he traced the outline of his father's name and dates, then down to follow the outline of the steam locomotive in the stone. Two or three times he trotted to the embankment to keep a restless Esther from rolling down onto the tracks. He suggested she hunt for red clovers in the grass, a short-lived distraction.

He laid a hand on the ground near the gravestone under which he imagined a responding heart. Esther's dwindling patience at last drew her to his side where she whined and fidgeted, eventually leaning on him to a tipping point. He arose to re-embrace the present. His eyes fell on the grave stones around him inscribed with names no doubt once known to his father. The air had the smell of rain about it so he gave Esther a piggyback ride to hasten their return to the car.

On the way into town he filled up at the two-pump gas station on Main Street. The attendant had an Esso emblem over one shirt pocket and the name "Bud" sewn over the other. "Do you still have a street called Short Street in town?" Paul asked.

Bud gestured with his head. "Up by the tracks. Go right out of here and take your first left up the hill. You'll think you're drivin' into a lumber yard, but that's where Short Street starts — on the other side of the lumber yard."

He turned south then up the hill to pass open storage sheds stacked with clapboards, trimmed lumber, two by fours and rough-cut planks. The car bumped across the rusting tracks and up a dead-end lane shaded with maples. There it was, third house up, gingerbread framing the wraparound porch right out of the old snapshots he'd been shown. There was the familiar bay window in which his mother's prized African violets were brought into bloom before being shared with the town library, church parlor, physician's office, and shut-ins' bedrooms around town. This day the window framed a vigorous red geranium stretching outward and upward between the window and a lacy curtain. He parked and let Esther out of the car. She headed for the homemade sandbox that crowned the unmown lawn. On that lawn his father had taken naps in the shade of a big maple now survived by a rotting stump. The oversized Old Glory that hung from the porch ceiling every Fourth was long gone, like his sister and his father. He wanted to walk onto the porch. If there had been someone at home he might be bold enough to ask, but the house and yard were quiet.

Before he lost the good western light he unzipped his camera case and snapped some shots from several angles, including Esther's crouched figure in as many as the light would allow. He decided not to intrude further. Lifting his petulant leg-flailing child from the sand he carried her down to the grade crossing where he knelt to run a finger over the rust-jacketed steel. What had he expected to find there? Nothing at all, he admitted to himself. Still. These are the very ties. Well, maybe not after thirty years. But probably the very ballast stones. The very rails. He couldn't prevent himself from imagining a child's tiny foot jammed in there. And a fire-breathing dragon roaring out of the curve now half hidden with elm saplings.

After dinner he sat in the inn's dining room reading the *Bennington Banner* as Esther fed Doll Baby French fries. Around them men and women spoke about whether they were planning to go "up" tonight. His mind went back to the story about the "legendary ghost train" he'd read in *Grit*.

Keeping his eye on Esther, he strolled to the front desk where the innkeeper sat making entries in a ledger. "What were those people talking about in the tavern just now?" he asked her.

She answered without looking up. "It's nothing really. Just talk. Not much to do in a small town, so they make up stories."

"Can you tell me the story?" She said nothing, continuing to work with the ledger. "I'm interested in trains," he said.

With a sigh she tossed the pen down. She stared across the counter at him. "The story is that there's a train that comes through here once in a while. They call it a "ghost train" and seem to enjoy hanging about all night up there in the lumber yard swatting mosquitoes and waiting for something to happen which mostly it doesn't. At least not for me." She went back to her ledger.

"Have you been up there with the others?"

"Twice was enough for me. I've got better fish to fry."

He sensed that her resignation had given way to irritation. She was no longer focused on trains — or on him.

He rejoined Esther, signed the dinner bill and scouted for a resident with more interest in the train or ghost or whatever it might be that had stirred this town. He took Esther's hand, pushed against the screen door and stepped out onto a full-length porch.

Two men stood in the shadows, cigarettes glowing at their raised fingertips. He recognized the man in the Blue Seal cap as one of those who had been inside earlier. The second one was "Bud," the man who had pumped gas for him. When he moved to where they stood their conversation stopped. He lifted Esther and Doll Baby into his arms.

"Excuse me," he said, putting a smile in his voice. "I couldn't help overhearing talk inside about a train that might come through town. Did I hear right?"

The men exchanged glances. Bud lowered his gaze. Blue Seal flicked the sparking remains of his cigarette out over the sidewalk. "Probably," he said.

"But the tracks through town are rusty," Paul said.

"Is there any pattern to it? A schedule?"

Bud gave a low chuckle. "What do you say, Bear? Is there a 'schedule'?"

Bear hesitated, frowning toward Bud. "Sort of," he said.

"Once a year," said Bud, "sometimes twice."

Paul waited.

Again the men looked at each other. Whatever passed between them in that moment increased his chances for an answer, because Bear looked toward the street. "Weather pretty much decides the schedule," he said. "Got to be foggy. Got to be late August. And got to be foggy."

Paul had followed his gaze to the street. Streetlights were ringed with a gathering haze as the night deepened. "Tonight could meet that description," he offered.

"Might could," said Bear.

"Do you think I might see it?"

"No telling."

"I mean, can outsiders see it?"

"Some do, some don't."

"Who does see it then? What kind of people?"

"All kinds!" Bud interrupted eagerly. "Well,... priests don't." He chuckled. "Or nuns." Paul remained silent, unsure whether his leg was being pulled. "Oh, and kids," added Bud. "Kids don't see it. People last year took their kids up to see it come by and the kids slept right through all the chugging and whistling. Figure that out!" he added, smirking at Bear in self-approval.

"Yeah," said Bear. "Your little one there wouldn't pay any attention to it."

"Hard to account for, ain't it?" said Bud. "People put pennies on the track up there all the time. Nothin' ever touches 'em. You'd think that train was tearin' up ground for all the commotion, but it never touches a penny."

"Where is it coming from," Paul asked, "and why through The Crossing?"

"You scratch anybody in this town," said Bear, "and you'll find a theory about that train."

Paul shifted Esther's weight to his shoulder where she began playing with his ear. "If I scratched you what theory would I find?" he asked Bear.

"If you were to ask me, it all has somethin' to do with the accident up there some thirty years back," said Bear.

"I second that," said Bud, leaning toward Paul for emphasis.

Paul grew light-headed. For support, he pressed against the clapboards on the front of the inn, securing himself against a window casing. "What can you tell me about that accident?" he asked.

Bud took up the question talking fast and loud, indicating to Paul a delight in the spotlight. "Little girl got runned over by a train one night up there. Terrible thing! I think this ghost is driven by the same engineer on that train. I'd bet the farm on it."

Bud shifted his hip to draw out a pouch of tobacco and unrolled it. "I'd say if anybody was to be haunted, it'd be that engineer," he said, nodding for emphasis. He pressed a wad of fibers between his gum and lip.

"Terrible accident!" agreed Bear. "Double terrible!"

"Why double?" asked Paul.

"Well! Was the girl's own father ran over her!"

Paul felt the blood drain from his face. He shuddered and crossed the porch to collapse on the railing with Esther's head on his shoulder. Gripping the porch pillar with his free hand, he held on. His words came in a hoarse breath.

"Do you know that for a fact?"

"Oh, that's known for sure," said Bear. "Wasn't more'n another five, six weeks and he was dead, too. Killed himself over it, everyone said. Stepped in front of a switch engine in the Bennington yards. The railroad company called it 'willful negligence' or some such."

Paul ached for his mother.

"Daddy, you're hurting me!" He relaxed his grasp on Esther. It had increased with each revelation.

He turned to look at the street, to see someone walking by, a shade being pulled, anything to return him to the real world. A car hissed past on the wet pavement.

"What about Esther?"

"Who?"

"The little girl. How did she get on the tracks?"

"The story I remember," said Bear, "was that when the night train would come through — they lived up there near the tracks, you could throw a lump of coal from the train and hit their house — when the train come through it would wake her up and she'd fuss and her mother'd have a time getting her back down. The woman got so she'd tell the little girl a story that the train whistles were just her daddy passin' by and sorta sayin' hello to her from the train at the foot of their street. 'Nothing to be afraid of,' she would tell her."

"Yeah," agreed Bud, "as long as she just listened to it from her crib."

"This one night," said Bear, "the mother fell asleep at her kitchen table."

The intimacy of that knowledge offended Paul and he challenged them. "How the hell would you guys know whether she was asleep or not?"

The men exchanged glances, shifted their stance. Paul's sudden change of tone appeared to baffle Blue Seal. A frown crossed his forehead, but he said nothing.

Bud decided to defend their interpretation of the accident. "Everybody in town knows that. Neighbors on Short Street said the woman admitted it. She just plain fell asleep at the table. Been working' all day... then... who knows? The kid took it into her head to go down the street and wave to her daddy."

Esther chose the moment to squirm her way to the porch floor. She began poking her face through each opening along the railing.

Bear kept his eyes on Paul as Bud's story unfolded. When next he spoke he softened his voice in contrast to his friend's performance.

He said to Paul, "The sheriff's department figured the little girl was probably doin' fine 'til the train rounded the curve and started coming toward her. The bright light and the loud whistle most likely startled her and she lost her footing. One leg got caught somehow. The more she pulled on it the tighter it wedged in. That's where me and my wife found her ten minutes later."

"Jesus!" Paul's voice was a whisper.

"She would have had almost no time to be afraid," Bear said, hoping to be right.

"I can't believe it!" said Paul. "Why? Why didn't the crew see her?"

"Oh, it was foggy," said Bear. "Fog comes right up off the river some nights. Can't see your hand in front of your face. It's a… it's like a whiteout in a snow storm. She had on a white nightie. Whatever the cause, you can bet that engineer would have given anything in the world for a second chance to roll through town that night."

Esther's meandering took her close enough to Bud to prompt his playful pat on her head. In a flash she wedged herself between her father's legs and the porch rails. He turned to pick her up.

"The poor fella was sick about it," said Bud, warming to the story. "When he got to the end of his run he collapsed when they pointed out the shreds of a child's nightgown on his engine and told him about the phone call they had got from Bear here. They took him to the hospital for overnight. He was in bad shape. Didn't go to work for a while. When he did go back the company took him off the mainline, gave him a make-work day job in the switch yard."

"There's no words in the language to say how bad you'd feel after that!" said Bear. "You just go around sayin' 'What if? What if?' She's saying, 'What if I hadn't canned so long? What if I hadn't told her the story about the damned whistles?' He's sayin', 'What if I'da slowed down more? What if we had bought her a red night gown.' You could play that game from now 'til the cows come home, but it don't bring nobody back."

"No," said Paul. "It don't bring nobody back."

The three were silent for several minutes. Paul felt Esther's breath against his ear.

"If a man wanted to see this train," he said at last, "where's the best vantage point?"

Bear motioned, lifting his elbow as if projecting it out beyond the inn. "You know where the lumber yard is?"

"Yeah."

"Right there."

"By Short Street?"

Bear absorbed the fact that this fellow wasn't all that much of a stranger to The Crossing. "Right there," he said again.

"When?"

"Around the time the old night train used to come through. Nine-thirty, ten, in there."

"Much obliged," said Paul. With that he and Esther moved back inside where he could see a clock. It was 8:30. He would leave in 45 minutes. Back in their room there was the musty smell of evening coolness. He changed Esther's damp diaper just in case, then slipped her into her night dress and drew the blanket over them as they lay on the bed. He told her stories of her grandfather that he had heard from his grandfather... about the trains, the big logs, about the animals that rode on his trains — cows and sheep and sometimes pigs oinking their way to market, which led to "this little piggy," which led to heavy eyelids and, finally, to sleep for Esther.

He stood by the window taking in the gathering darkness, watching the fog curl around the streetlight. He felt as alive as he had ever been, on the cusp of something, expectant but not apprehensive. He glanced over at his Esther in her white nightgown. He reached into his pocket to pull out his father's railroad watch on its brass chain. He held it up to his ear and shook it. The grain of rice was still inside. "It's not gold," his grandfather had told him. "Gold was for retirement." He gathered the brass chain against the watch, slipped it once again into his pocket and lay down next to Esther to wait.

He projected their day onto the water-stained ceiling above: his father's grave, the old homestead, the Short Street crossing, Bear's words about second chances. Then a train appearing as in his dreams. Was it on some sort of schedule? he had asked. An anniversary? Not for his sister's death anyway. More like his Esther's birthday if anything.

Esther's birthday?

Esther! My God — it's got to be Esther — he's trapped in his locomotive waiting for Esther! Bear was right: "...playing 'what if' don't bring nobody back." What if it's not about bringing anybody back, but about sending somebody on? He turned to look at his sleeping child. It's Esther he wants! He checked his watch... 8:45.

As all this coalesced in his head, he rushed to the sink and splashed cold water on his face. He now remembered the story in Grit. And the men on the porch told him children don't experience the train. Of course! It's parents he wants to come. And not just any parent. "She can't see it," he said aloud. "She won't see it!" He checked his watch. Ten of nine. He'd have to be there by nine-fifteen! No time to lose. He'd get himself ready before disturbing Esther. She could put up a fuss.

He shrugged into his jacket, pulling the car keys out of the pocket to make sure he had them. He leaned over the bed to scoop up Esther, blanket and all. Only when he began to lift her did his nose warn him that he was going to lose time.

"Shit!" He released the blanket and stood upright beside the bed. "Jesus, Louise, do they do that in their sleep?" His mind raced, focusing first on wrapping

119

the little figure in the blanket and in her coat, hurrying to the car and cleaning her up later. He abandoned it as soon as he pictured Louise discovering the ugly red rash on the little bottom tomorrow.

"Shit!" again. More roughly than he had intended he rolled the child this way and that, removing the offending diaper. He washed her bottom with the bathroom hand towel. He broke a sweat. He grew clumsy in his race to be done. What comes next? Powder. He shook white onto Esther's midsection. "Now a diaper!" — He rummaged the tote again — nothing soft there — carry bag to the lamp — hold it open — peer in. "No diaper." he said aloud. "Why no diaper, Louise?" Had she counted wrong? Had he used them all up in one day? Now his watch said 9:05 and up there at the crossing, something that could save his desperate father would soon disappear as he stood there yelling "Shit!" He had to make a diaper.

He took a desperate inventory of the room. Towel? Too thick. Handkerchief? Too thin. Curtains? Window shades? Bed sheets? He stopped there because it was the right color. He dare not look at his watch. What white did they bring? Yes! He shrugged off his jacket, tugged his sweater over his head, tore at his shirt to pop all the buttons onto the worn carpeting. He lifted the sweaty tee shirt from his back and held it before him. Holding it upside down he lay it atop the fussing figure, thrusting legs through the arm holes. He pulled the sides together over tummy and bum, securing their meeting place with a fat granny knot. Sweat ran down his chin and into her hair. He tried to sit her upright, but the improvised diaper tipped her to one side when he sat her up. He forced her blanket under her recumbent form to swaddle her as best he could. He drew the cold jacket over his bare shoulders, cupped the drowsy child off the bed, out the door and down the hall to the stairs. Once on the main floor he patted his right trouser pocket to be certain. No keys. Left pocket? No keys. Back up the staircase, along the corridor to their room where he found the keys on the dresser next to where he had taken them out to be sure he had them. He ran downstairs and out to the car on the fog-shrouded street. His headlights filled the windshield with reflected light.

In the lumber yard he pulled to what he hoped was the side of the street. He rolled down his window to listen, but heard only katydids calling from the weeds in what sounded to Paul like shared desperation. "Hear that, Esther?" he whispered. "They're calling to each other," he said. Then from somewhere in the darkness came the keening of a steam whistle.

He opened his door, walked around the car to open that door. The dome light glowed weakly on Esther trying to burrow herself back to sleep. He unhooked her from her car seat, gathered the nightgown around her to lift her out and into his arms. He leaned back in to retrieve her blanket then closed the door. He stood holding her, as the first glow appeared among the leaves of doomed elm saplings crowding the right of way. Again the cries of the oncoming locomotive echoed from the hills.

His mouth went dry. For the first time he allowed himself to admit what he proposed to do. "If she can't see the train," he reasoned, "no harm. But, suppose it doesn't stop? Even if it doesn't exist. Will it hit her? It doesn't flatten pennies, but… still."

Rays of light probed the fog. He shifted a squirming bundle to his other arm, checking to be sure the blanket still hung from his grip. The train's fogbound wail was muffled but no less insistent. He heard softened voices from across the tracks. The ground throbbed under him. The oncoming clamor filled the yard. His child registered nothing more than her impatience to be put back to bed. He shuffled across the all but invisible ground, clutching Esther, the blanket trailing beside him. He tripped on the near rail of the siding, forcing himself to plant one foot in front of the other until his shoe hit the track of the mainline.

The locomotive, its coal tender, the first tank cars swayed around the curve and bore down on them. The glow from the firebox in the cab outlined the silhouette of the engineer leaning from the cab window — straining, determined, his body half out of the opening as his eyes searched the swirling fog, his round, steel-rimmed glasses reflecting the firebox.

Paul's heart pounded, his hands trembled as he bent to drape the small blanket between the rails. He lowered a whining Esther onto it only to discover her clenched fist locked on his jacket sleeve. "Damn," he said aloud, "why didn't I bring Doll Baby?" The locomotive groaned and clanked toward them. With his free hand he reached into his pocket to pull out his father's watch He swung it by the chain in front of her face, lowering it until she released his jacket to wrap her fingers around the chain. As she did so her makeshift diaper canted her to her right. He moved to stabilize her, thought better of it and backed away, his heels probing for obstacles behind him. Within three steps he saw that if he did not know where he had placed her he never could have found her again. He backed once more then anchored himself preparing to pounce, leaning forward, tensing the leg muscles, spreading his hands, as the train bore its ponderous way toward the little figure between the rails.

A sudden breath of air chilled the back of his head. The fog, once static, now eddied on the tracks. A breeze crossed the river, bringing the outline of the oncoming locomotive into sharper focus. He braced himself.

"Oh, my God!" a woman shouted from some-where on his left.

He had been seen.

The locomotive lurched along the far lumber sheds when the leaning engineer stiffened in recognition. He lunged back into the cab to cut power and yank on his air brake. The sound from the smokestack changed pitch and the drive wheels began to grab.

Once more the figure returned to the window as if to gauge the distance. Again into the cab, now dumping all the air in the brakes. He yanked a lever to send sand pouring onto the rails as the massive drive wheels locked in place and scraped a shower of hot sparks toward the child. The added friction ground the locomotive to a standstill from where Paul, had he reached out, could have touched the front coupling.

A small, tentative group appeared from the sheds and pressed forward to take advantage of the sudden calm. Leading them, hand in hand with a woman, was Bear. The locomotive loomed over them, coughing black smoke, vents hissing pent-up steam into the lifting fog. Paul strode past the drive wheels to peer into the cab where the engineer slumped on his seat, spectacles in one hand, a bandana at his face, his body rocking back and forth inside the open window. Paul hoisted Esther to his shoulders forgetting there was nothing for her to see. Spectators crowded behind him.

The engineer replaced his spectacles. He reached for the throttle. The drive wheels slipped then caught the gritty rails to ease the train forward, jerking each car behind as the couplings took up the slack. The locomotive clanked past Paul and Esther, its stack funneling smoke into the night, the engineer focusing once more on the tracks ahead.

The train rumbled past until the ponderous locomotive rolled onto the bridge. At mid river the engineer turned to look back along the length of his train, prompting a gasp from the onlookers.

Paul whispered, "Wave, Esther." She raised her hand toward she knew not what and opened and closed her palm as the locomotive rounded the curve dragging its cars one by one until the glow of red lanterns winked out. "Bye bye, train," said Paul.

He turned then to see the parents, young and ancient, by the hazy light from the street lamp. Bear stood there, his arm around the woman.

"Who are you?" said Bear.

"Where did you come from?" said Althea.

THE 7:02 TRAIN TO
BELLOWS FALLS

Iris, the pretty waitress at the Blue Benn Diner, was telling me about her brother Carl who worked for *The Town Crier*, a weekly newspaper over in Bellows Falls. The editor called him in one day. "I'd like you to go up to St. Albans to cover the Native American pow wow this weekend. Take some pictures and write enough copy to hold the pictures together so our readers will understand what happens at a pow wow." Carl rode the train up to St. Albans, made a lot of notes, took a bunch of pictures and returned to the St. Albans train station for the return trip to Bellows Falls. He had a few minutes to kill, so he walked over to one of those scales that invited one to: Deposit a quarter and learn your accurate weight and fortune.

Carl stepped onto the scale and slid a quarter into the slot. The machine rumbled and shook and spit out a little piece of cardboard with printing on it: You are a white male, you weigh 185 pounds and you are holding a ticket for the 7:02 train to Bellows Falls. All true, but Carl couldn't figure out how the machine knew he was white and what his ticket read. Could it be that accurate twice in a row? He dug into his pocket, pulled out another quarter, shoved it into the slot and waited. The machine jiggled and groaned and spit out this little piece of cardboard. He pulled it outto read: You are a white male, you weigh 185 pounds, in your pocket is a ticket for the 7:02 train to Bellows Falls.

Carl looked around for hidden cameras. He studied the face of the ticket seller looking for evidence of a grin. Nothing there. He studied the others waiting for trains. His gaze fell on an American Indian wearing a full-feathered headdress.

He approached the Indian and asked, "Sir, would you mind coming over here and getting weighed? I'll pay the quarter. I just want to see what your fortune is."

The Indian agreed. He went over to stand on the scale. Carl pulled out his next to last quarter and put it in the slot. The scale shook and grunted then spit out a piece of cardboard. Carl read it: You are a full-blooded American Indian, you weigh 202 pounds and you're holding a ticket for the 7:30 train to Montreal. The Indian went back to sit down and Carl was left scratching his head. He reached in his pocket where he had one quarter left. He walked back to the Indian, but this time he said, "Can I borrow your headdress?"

The Indian carefully handed Carl the headdress. "Don't drop it," he said, "whatever you do." He adjusted it carefully on Carl's head. Carl made his way to the scale, one hand on the headdress. He stepped onto the scale, inserted his last quarter and waited for the bump and groan to cease. A piece of cardboard popped out: You are a white male. You weigh 192 pounds with an Indian headdress on, and you have just missed the 7:02 train to Bellows Falls.

THE MAN WHO CLUNG TO EARTH

In the Mettawee River Valley of Vermont dairy farmers are blessed with rich bottom land from the Mettawee River. One old man worked a dwindling dairy herd on what had once been his great-grandfather's farm. The old man so loved those meadows, wood lots, and hills where he hunted that he almost never left the farm. They got him up to the state fair in Rutland one year. He never went back. Said he'd already seen it.

He thought, with some justification, that there was no place in the world as much like heaven as the Mettawee River Valley.

As sometimes happens with people when they get old and very sick — they have a feeling that they are about to die. The day that premonition came to the old man he told his sons that his last wish was to be carried out of the house and laid next to the river where he could hear it flowing by.

His sons carried him out to the edge of a cornfield by the river. The old man laid his hand on the soil and, with his last breath, closed his fist over it. He died a happy man. The next thing he knew he was standing outside Heaven's gate. St. Peter came out to greet him. "Welcome," he said. "Been waitin' on you. Come in."

"Yes, thank you, I will," said the old man moving toward those big gates.

Just then St. Peter lay his hand on the old man's chest and gestured at his clenched fist. "I'm sorry," he said. "You can't come into Heaven while you're still clinging to Earth."

The man looked down, opened his fingers and saw what was there. "Can't leave that," he said. "That's good Mettawee bottom land. This was my daddy's before me. And my granddaddy's before him and my great granddaddy's. No, no, I'm not going to give that up."

"Well, you can't come into Heaven while you're still clinging to Earth." St. Peter went in without him. The old man sat outside the gate for an eon or so.

Naturally this came to the attention of God and she decided to do something about it. She put on one of her favorite disguises. She wore a long, white beard; made herself into a man; had a long, white gown, sandals... that costume. She went out to talk to the old man. He knew who she was — he'd seen her picture. "Don't you want to come in?" she said to him. "You've a place in Heaven. You were good to your family, you were good to your help, you were kind to your animals. You've earned the right to come in."

"Yes," he said. "I want to come in."

God offered her arm and together they walked up to the gates but when they got there God put her hand out on his chest. She said, "First you've got to let go of what you have in your hand."

The old man opened his hand. "Oh, no," he said, "I can't do that. That's good Mettawee bottom land. You're the one who gave it to us. This soil fed us and let me be good to my animals and to my help and to my family. No, no. I can't let that go."

"I'm sorry," she said, "but you can't be clinging to Earth when you come into Heaven." God went back through the gates and the old man sat down again.

After an eon or so God decided to have another go at it, this time dressing up as one of the old man's hunting buddies. She donned a Day-Glo orange cap, shrugged on a red-and-black wool jacket, and pulled on a pair of mukluks over her pant legs. On her way out she grabbed a pinochle deck. They were playing cards when she said, "Everybody but you is in camp. Don't you want to see all your old buddies? They've all said they're not going to shave until you get into camp. Some of them are beginning to look a little ratty."

The old man grinned. "Believe I'll come in just to listen to their lies."

So they got up, God slipped the pinochle deck in her jacket, and as they approached the gates God reached over to put her hand on the old man's chest once again. "There's a new camp rule," she said. "Everybody agreed to let go of Earth before they came in." With that she gestured toward his closed fist.

The man opened his hand again to see what was there. "Don't you know what this is?" he asked. "This is good Mettawee soil here. It is this soil that holds the track of the deer so we can track 'em to feed the family. You're a hunter. You should know that; you can't just throw something like that away. No, I'm not going to do that." So God went back through the gates and the man went and sat down again, for another eon or so.

God decided to try one more time. This time she went out disguised as this old man's little granddaughter — seven, maybe eight years old. She put a pink bow in her hair; she put on black, patent-leather Mary Janes; she wore a white dress with little eyelets in it and went out skipping to where he sat and leaned on his knee. She looked up into his eyes. "Grandpa," she said, "aren't you going to come in with us? Everybody's around the table except you, Grandpa. There's no one to say grace. Your chair is empty."

He tried to stand up, but he had been out there a few eons so he had the arthritis pretty bad. He was struggling to get over there to the gate when the little girl said to him, "Grandpa, hold my hand and I'll help you through."

When the old man reached for his granddaughter's hand all that dry, dusty soil from the Mettawee Valley filtered out. He took her hand and together they walked through that big gate. Once inside the old man looked around and fell to his knees because there he was — standing on the banks of the Mettawee.

DEER EYES
A Drama

The curtain comes up on a darkened stage. Stage lights come up slowly, as a dawn might, to reveal a man and a woman facing the audience. Two grave stones lie facing them. The man, of middle age, stands before one grave stone. He is of medium build, wearing ill-fitting black trousers supported by suspenders and a belt too long for his waist. His well-worn soiled white shirt is open at the neck with the sleeves rolled up. The high cuffs of the trousers let us see white ankle socks under scuffed black dress shoes. He appears self conscious, fixing on each thought as it occurs to him. The woman is dressed for office work in sharply creased slacks and crisp white blouse. She kneels before a nearby grave stone. In one gloved hand she holds a potted geranium, in the other a garden trowel.

WILLIE, *gazing at the sky*: I think it's going to change, Mrs. Darcy. When you see high, thin clouds like that, it means the weather is going to change. *When he gets no response he hurries on.* Do you know you can see whole family trees here in this cemetery? If you look up there on the hillside, *pointing over the heads of the audience,* and you went around and figured out all the begats on those tombstones, you could see whole family trees there.

MRS. DARCY, *without looking up*: That's right, Willie.

WILLIE, *earnestly*: Mrs. Darcy, would you mind calling me Will? I'd be in your debt.

MRS. DARCY: Of course, Willie, if that's what you'd like.

WILLIE: Well, thank you. People call me Willie. That was all right when I was a little boy but now I'm grown up; I'm a thirty-eight-year-old man, and people still call me Willie: momma, my uncle, my cousins, the awful — the neighbors across the street from where I live, people at work, even papa, before he died.

Mrs. Darcy, having listened, returns to her planting.

I ask people to call me Will and they say, "No, Willie's your name. You're special." I don't want to be special. I didn't ask to be special, Mrs. Darcy. I just want to be regular. I hope you don't think of me as special, Mrs. Darcy.

Mrs. Darcy tilts her head slightly toward him as if to consider. After a pause she decides not to answer.

I like your geraniums. They really… they grow fast and they last long, don't they Mrs. Darcy? I could, if you like, I could tend your geraniums since I'm here most every day. I could bring water from the tap and I could water 'em, and I could deadhead 'em. I learned that. I learned about gardening from papa.

Papa taught me about gardening and about how to weed. You got to pick the broccoli before the little yellow flowers come out. *He hurries on.* I'm here most every day.

MRS. DARCY, *sits back on her heels to wipe her forehead with the back of her gloved hand*: Do you always come this early?

WLLIE: Well, I'm coming from work.

MRS. DARCY: Do you work at the mill?

WILLIE: No, no, I don't work there, I work up in Rutland.

Silence.

In a restaurant.

MRS. DARCY: Are you a cook?

WILLIE: Oh, no, I clean it.

MRS. DARCY, *pauses to reflect*: I see.

WILLIE: I get there about 11 o'clock and then I'm there cleaning all night long and then I get through and drive back home and get back here in the morning about when everybody else is going to work. So I stop just about every day.

Silence.

Hastening to fill the silence. I hope it's a job that's going to last because a lot of the jobs I've had in the past couple or three years, they've all been jobs they say they're going to need me. After a while they say they don't need me, and sometimes, sometimes I have to quit.

MRS. DARCY: What would make you quit?

WILLIE: Well, because they're not nice. Or they're not completely honest, if you know what I mean.

Silence.

Again, to fill the silence: You've got nice tools there. Papa left some tools but they're not nice and new like yours are. I learned a lot from papa just being in the garden with him. He wouldn't exactly let me be in the garden. Papa said it was easier for him and quicker if he could just do it himself and not bother to teach anybody.

Silence.

I sat on the ground outside the garden. And, then, when I was real little, Mrs. Darcy, when I was little and he would be away at work I'd lie between the rows in the garden. I made myself real skinny and I would just lie there. He put strings where he was going to plant the lettuce over here and where he was going to plant, you know, radishes, carrots, or something over there. I learned a lot from papa just by watching and not touching the strings. Still, I feel like there's something that papa forgot to teach me.

MRS. DARCY: What would that be?

WILLIE: It's hard to explain. It's like he didn't teach me how to do life. How to fit in. How to be places or just be with people. And I think papa just forgot to teach me that. Other people, people like you, Mrs. Darcy, you're somebody. You can — you go to work and you go to church, and you're in clubs, I bet. See, it's like people's papas taught them those things and then it just comes back to them when they need it. But now, (*pause*) I don't know, I'm kind of afraid with papa gone. It's like there's something that he just didn't tell me. He maybe didn't have time to tell me. Maybe papa will get up in Heaven and he'll look down and he'll see me down here next to his grave and he'll say, "By golly, there's Willie and he's down there and there's one thing I forgot to tell him." Then he'll come down and he'll tell me. Or, maybe, Mrs. Darcy, maybe God would send him back. God would be up there and He'd be looking down here at the graveyard and He'd say, "Albert, with all the things you showed that boy of yours, there's one thing you didn't show him. You go back down there and show him." (*Pause*) That's why I come every morning. I'm afraid if I don't come that will be the one day he'll come and I won't know. I come even when it rains but I don't get out of the car.

MRS. DARCY: Well, at least you have come, Will.

WILLIE: Does that sound silly to you, Mrs. Darcy?

MRS. DARCY: Not at all.

WILLIE: Well, sometimes it does even to me. I don't know what I'll do if momma dies. Momma and Corporal Stewart, they — Corporal Stewart is the State Trooper who comes when I call up about the awful people across the street from us. He comes and we sit outside in his cruiser and talk. Well, anyway, momma and Corporal Stewart, they want me to go back to county counseling, but I'm not going to. *(With emphasis)* I don't think they're nice people. If you ever get into trouble, don't you go to them.

MRS. DARCY: I'll have to remember that.

WILLIE: Still, I wish I had somebody to talk to; I just wish I had somebody I could talk to and have them listen to me and have 'em believe me. Like, if I just had a young woman. I bet you know young women at your church, don't you? If there's a young woman in your church maybe who might want to be companionable with me?"

MRS. DARCY: What do you mean by that, Will?

WILLIE: Oh, no, Mrs. Darcy. I don't mean anything by that. If I offend, I'm sorry. I just was thinking about some-body …maybe at work. You know a lot of people at work, I bet. I bet there might be a woman who needs somebody to be companionable. I'm talking about going out for a snack or to a movie. When papa got real sick I just know that he was sad he didn't have any grandchil-dren or didn't have any prospects of grandchildren. What with Frankie gone and everything and me not being settled with a woman he didn't think he had any chance of being a grandfather. I felt bad about that. His card-playing friends had 'em — grandchildren. Yes, I could hear 'em bragging on their grandchildren to papa. Telling how they taught them where the trout are, and how to stack wood so it would air dry, and how to plant straight rows in the garden, how to clean a rifle. Or, just take 'em to the State Fair, or go to their school programs. But papa didn't have that prospect. When Frankie got killed — at Frankie's funeral I heard papa tell somebody that that was the end of our family.

MRS. DARCY, *slowly turns toward him in consolation*: Oh, Willie.

WILLIE: It didn't have to be if I'd had somebody to be companionable with when papa died.

MRS. DARCY, *searching for something encouraging to say*: I like the stone you picked out for your father.

WILLIE, *quickly adjusting*: Thank you, that's a complement. It's just a small one. It's just got room on it for his name and dates. I actually wanted to put a line from a poem on it. If you look at it, there isn't any room for that but I thought maybe it would be nice to put a line from a poem on it. But momma said every time they put another letter on it it costs more. Did you know that?

Silence.

Well, I didn't. And then she said it would have to be a bigger stone if it had something else on it. And it would cost even more, and she just said 'no.' I wrote a poem about papa and me. I read it at his funeral. Were you at his funeral?

MRS. DARCY: No, I couldn't be there.

WILLIE: That's all right. No, I understand. Well, anyway, I read this poem at papa's funeral. I wrote it about a time when he took me up into Sunderland. He used to hunt there. Yes, and we went up there where he used to hunt. We went up this dirt road, and we went around and went south there, just like we were going up the Green

Mountains but we didn't. Then we went to a place where we had to get out of the car and then we had to walk down a deer trail and we came down and then the next thing I knew, Mrs. Darcy, we were in this wonderful room — it was all pine trees on the ceiling and all pine needles on the floor, just like tree-to-tree carpeting. It was so nice in there, and then he told me to lie down there and I laid down right where he pointed and then he laid down right next to me and we could look out and we could see the whole valley out there. We could see the cars coming and going and the Wilcox Dairy trucks going back and forth to the dairy, and Equinox Mountain over there, Red Mountain over there — it was just so wonderful in there. Papa said there would be deer in there sometimes during the day. When they were resting they'd be in there. I said to papa, "We can come up here with sleeping bags and sleep in here." And he said we could.

MRS. DARCY: That sounds like a good idea.

WILLIE: We never went back there. *Picking up where he had left off.* Anyway, I wrote a poem about that; that's the poem I read at papa's funeral. In the poem we were in our cozy outdoor pine room only this time we were two deer. We looked out and saw the whole world out there, everybody. But they couldn't see us. They didn't know we were up there. We just looked out like deer. We didn't have to do anything that had to do with the world. That was a good afternoon. *He pauses in thought.* Papa could have told me right then what it was he forgot to. He was kind of quiet that day I think we missed a chance for him to give me a lesson about doing life.

Mrs. Darcy looks over at him, but says nothing.

WILLIE, *back again in the present*: Is that car new? Do you like foreign cars?

MRS. DARCY: My husband said they are well made.

WILLIE: That's what they say about them. Boy, papa would never drive a car that wasn't made in this country, even if he could save money. And papa was particular about saving money. Papa told me that I was conceived in a $7 bed. He said it had a spring broke, and he would tell that to the fellas playing cards downstairs and they would all laugh at that. I could hear momma saying to them, "Now be quiet or the boy will hear." I always did hear. One time one of papa's friends was playing cards and said papa should have named me Edsel — they all laughed at that too. It made me all hot and prickly inside. It was like the time in junior high when I was left back a grade and the kids started calling me Slow Willie. That ended something in me. I just lost my curiosity there in junior high.

MRS. DARCY: I'm sorry to hear that.

WILLIE: I used to be curious in school. I wanted to know everything. Then I just wasn't curious any more. I just lost all that.

MRS. DARCY: Did you stay in school?

WILLIE: I did through eleventh grade, but it wasn't any fun any more. After Frankie was killed, Mrs. Darcy, when Frankie was killed I thought momma and papa would love me all the more. They would need me all the more because I was all they had left. But it didn't work out that way. They just were angry with me all the time. It was as though I couldn't do anything right for them.

Mrs. Darcy stops her work, but can't bring herself to look at him.

WILLIE, *his practiced resilience restored, looks offstage toward her car*: That's a roomy trunk you have. Boy, you could carry — I see you've got a bag of peat moss. I have peat moss at home. I used it just day before yesterday. I planted a little maple tree in our front yard. I put peat moss all around it so when I mow the lawn, I won't bump the tree. It tells me where the roots are and I won't cut 'em. A maple tree has a big leaf, Mrs. Darcy, did you know that? Even when it is a sapling the leaves are already grown up. Then, in the fall they will turn beautiful colors and all. And when it gets big enough, I'll tap it.

MRS. DARCY: It will take some growing up before you can do that.

WILLIE: I know that. *He shades his eyes and looks up the hill over the heads of the audience.* I wish papa, before he died, had bought a plot up there on the hillside. See how up there there's trees shading all those graves. I wish he'd bought up there. Instead he let it all go and momma and I bought this plot down here. There's no trees in this section. That's why the grass is all burnt up. It's terrible down here. If he'd been up there, you and I could be shady right now. *He points up the hill.* You see those oak trees up there, Mrs. Darcy? Now, I admire those. Do you admire oak trees?

MRS. DARCY: I suppose I do, Will. I've never thought about it.

WILLIE: They don't drop their leaves off in the fall when

other trees do. They keep 'em on way into winter. Still, they're all dead. It's as if God didn't teach 'em to just let go. They have got to let go sometime otherwise they couldn't have new leaves. I'm going to look and see, you know, do they all fall on the same day or do they just all drop off when they get tired? Why do you never see an oak tree out in the middle of a meadow, Mrs. Darcy? You see elms out in a field sometimes.

MRS. DARCY, *beginning to pick up her belongings around the grave stone*: The elms are all pretty much gone now.

WILLIE: I mean when they were living you would see them out in the middle of a meadow. And sometimes you'd see a maple out in the middle and you'll see cows under it sitting in the shade but you never see an oak tree. Why do you suppose that is?

MRS. DARCY: Their seeds are not windblown. They drop their acorns right next to the parent tree.

WILLIE: That could be it! It's like the big ones are the papas and the little ones are the babies and the babies have to stay with the big ones who protect them until they are grown up.

MRS. DARCY: It takes many years before an oak tree is grown up.

WILLIE, *as if to himself*: They grow slow. They're … slow.

MRS. DARCY: Yes, Will.

WILLIE: By golly! That's special. *With excitement*, I wonder, Mrs. Darcy, do you think they would let me bring an oak tree down here and put it in this section? One of those little saplings that doesn't belong to anybody, I don't think. Would I have to ask somebody before I plant it? Who would I —

MRS. DARCY: I imagine you would have to talk to the Cemetery Commission.

WILLIE: Oh, a Commission! Oh, no, I don't think I would want to ask a Commission. Could you? Could you ask about it for me?

MRS. DARCY, *allowing her sigh to be observed*: I don't know, Willie —

WILLIE: I'd be in your debt, Mrs. Darcy. That would be something, wouldn't it? As that tree grew up it would send roots underground and something of papa where he's buried and the root would soak it up and it would go up in the trunk like it was sap or blood or something. And it would get up there and then when the tree was big enough it would have baby acorns and then those acorn babies would be taken by squirrels. You know, I don't believe Mrs. Darcy that a squirrel always knows where he's hidden his acorns. So I bet you that if he were to hide a lot of acorns around in this lower part of this meadow that he wouldn't find them all and they would grow into little oak trees. Wouldn't that be something!"

MRS. DARCY: A small tree will need lots of care, Will.

WILLIE: Oh, I would baby it. I would water it. I'd wrap the trunk against rabbits. There could be oak trees around here long after I was gone.

MRS. DARCY, *looks at her watch*: Oh, my! I need to go to work.

WILLIE: Sure, you go into town. I'm just going to say goodbye to papa, so you go on into town. Thank you for speaking with me, Mrs. Darcy. You're a real friend.

MRS. DARCY *moves off stage toward her car carrying her tools*: Goodbye, Will.

WILLIE, *calling after her*: Don't forget about the Commission and the tree. Oh, and a young woman? Don't forget about a young — *He pauses than adds*: Bye, Mrs. Darcy. *Then softly*: God bless you. *Willie turns back to look down toward his father's gravestone*: Papa? Can you hear me? I think, papa, if you've been trying to come back here and tell me something I don't think it's going to work. I'm not hearing you, papa. That's all right. You go back and rest. I don't think I'm going to be coming back as often as I did, but I won't leave you alone, papa. I'm going to bring you a tree. I'm going to plant a small oak tree here, papa. *He raises his face to look heavenward*: And if that tree gets killed, I'll put another tree in its place. And if that tree comes up bent or crooked, I'll take that one out and I'll put in another tree. I'll keep putting trees in here, papa, until I get one that's tall and strong and one you can be proud of.

BLACKOUT

THE BAKED BEANS

When I hear bad music, it makes me think of baked beans. Baked beans makes me think of Boston. Boston makes me think of Bucky Grimm. Bucky got the idea to go into business for himself while he was in Boston at the funeral of his Aunt Elvira.

He drove down the day of the funeral and decided to stay overnight. He went into the Hotel Spencer down there. The desk clerk said, "At the moment we have no rooms available, but earlier this afternoon a long-time resident of ours passed away. His room should be ready in another hour if you'd like to get some dinner first." Bucky said that was fair enough and he settled at a table in the hotel dining room.

A waiter came over to tell him about the house special: Boston Baked Beans. Bucky heard him out then said simply, "I'll have a hamburger."

The waiter said, "Don't you like baked beans?"

Bucky said, "I like 'em, but I'm going to have a hamburger."

The waiter went away. A couple of minutes later the dining room manager came over to say, "What's the matter with baked beans for dinner? People come here from all over the country to get our house specialty."

Bucky pushed his chair back to look up. "Are you out of hamburger?" he asked.

"No, sir, but our baked beans are exceptionally good."

Bucky was getting a mite peeved at all this baked beans business. "Look," he said, "if I can't get what I want here, I'll go someplace where I can." A couple minutes later Bucky had a hamburger.

Walking across the lobby after supper, he saw the desk clerk beckon him over. He had him sign the register and gave him his room key. On his way to the elevator Bucky stopped at a rack of newspapers from cities around the country. He looked up and down the rack but couldn't see what he was looking for. He went up to the desk clerk. "I'm looking for the *Bennington Banner*."

"The … I don't even know where Bennington is."

"Well, I wouldn't admit it," said Bucky. "Everyone in Bennington knows where Boston is."

Later that night Bucky got into bed, turned out the light and got under the covers. He was just dozing off when the door opened and a woman came in, all dressed in white. She walked over to Bucky's bed. Without turning on the light, she tore the covers off Bucky, rolled him over, pulled the pajamas off his butt and jabbed a hypodermic needle into the fat of his behind.

In the morning when he complained he was told the woman was a nurse to the old man, but nobody had told her that the old man died.

Nowadays if Bucky Grimm hears you're going to Boston he'll warn you. "If you stay at the Hotel Spencer and you eat dinner there — whatever you do — don't refuse the baked beans."

THE GOOD LOOKIN' SUIT

Bucky returned from Boston convinced that the best work a man could find would be undertaking. His Aunt Elvira's funeral had illustrated for him how few skills are required other than common courtesy. He knew you had to deal with the body and he figured he'd hire a young person out of mortuary school for that — maybe a woman, save himself some money. Everything else he saw involved opening and closing doors of big black cars, greeting people at the front of the funeral home and talking in hushed tones. He didn't need to buy an expensive hearse; he already had a vehicle. Bucky had been a rubbish hauler the previous two years. He bought a couple gallons of black paint for his pickup truck. And one of those plastic magnetic signs. When he got a call he'd slap that sign onto the driver's side door. Very simple, it just said:

GRIMM
FUNERALS

He noticed all the men working Elvira's funeral wore black suits, something he didn't own. He shopped around Bennington to see what he could find. No one carried anything he could try on. He had an appointment with a monument firm up in Burlington. While he was up there he drove downtown and found a store with a half-price clearance sale on men's suits. He found a suit that fit him, but it wasn't black.

"This suit," said the salesman, "is a perfect fit for you and it's half price today. It's a deep navy which would be taken for black by anyone with normal eyesight. In fact, we couldn't move this suit because everyone we showed it to said, "No, this is black and I want blue."

Bucky felt he could not do better and the price was right. "I'll take it," he said.

"Take it off," said the salesman, "and I'll put it on a hanger for you."

Bucky looked at his watch. "I want to get home before dark, so just put my other clothes in a bag and I'll wear this one home."

He paid for the suit and left the store with his bag of old clothes. He had left his truck in a parking garage down the street. He turned right out of the store and promptly ran into an old friend who now lived in Burlington. After a minute of "How's the wife" talk he put his arms out and slowly spun around so the man could see the suit. "What do you think?" he asked. "It's a new suit. I got it for half price."

"Nice outfit," said his friend. "But the right sleeve is longer than the left sleeve."

"Yeah," said Bucky, looking closely, "I never noticed that. Glad I ran into you." Bucky returned to the store to find the salesman who had sold him the suit. "There's a problem with this suit I just bought. The right sleeve comes down farther over my wrist than the left one.

The clerk checks it out. "By golly," he said, "you're right. It was cut wrong. But that's a good-looking suit and the only one of its color I had. Tell you what you do: you pull that right sleeve up until the two cuffs are the same length. Then press your right arm firmly against your right side and no one will ever notice because that's a good-looking suit."

Bucky weighed the cost of the suit, his search for that color, and his desire to be on his way home and said, "Okay, I'll do that," and out he walked.

He turned right to pick up his truck when out of the doorway of a shop comes another fellow Bucky knew in Burlington. More "How's the wife" talk until Bucky takes a slow spin of pride and says, "New suit, what do you think. Got it just now for half price."

The other guy said, "Not bad for the price except for the left lapel."

"What's the matter with it?"

"Maybe it's just me, but it looks like there's too much material in it that makes it droop."

Bucky turned to his reflection in a store window. "I see what you mean. I'm glad I ran into you," and he walked back to the menswear store.

"I just discovered another problem," he told the clerk. "Look at how the left lapel droops."

The clerk looked at it. "By golly," he said, "you're right. Too much fabric there. But that's a good-looking suit. Tell you what you do. You keep one hand tight to your side to keep that sleeve in place, then you look in a mirror and with your other hand move that lapel just how you want it. Now, press your chin down on that side to keep the lapel in place. No one will notice it because that's such a good-looking suit."

Bucky was now worried about the time passing and number of miles before he gets home, so he thanked the clerk and headed out the door with his right arm tight at his side and his chin holding the left lapel in place. Just before he got to the corner he ran into a third guy he knew in Burlington. More "How's the wife, etc."

Bucky did his spin saying, "New suit. Half price. Whatdya think?"

"Nice, Bucky, but did you want the pants like that?"

"Like what?"

"Baggy like that. The cuffs almost cover the toes of your shoes, makes you look like a fourteen-year-old."

Bucky headed back up the street and into the store. "Look at these pants!" he said. "They're cut too long. Makes me look like a teenager."

"By golly, you're right," said the salesman, "But this suit looks good on you. Tell you what you do: You keep that one arm up tight to your torso, keep your chin down on that errant lapel and carefully reach down with your free hand and lift up the crotch with your thumb and pointer finger until your cuffs are right where you like them. No one will notice anything because that's a good-looking suit."

Bucky left the store again and headed toward the covered garage. He reached the corner and started across the street. Because he could not see the curb clearly he began to search it out by probing for it with his toes.

On the opposite corner stood two medical students from the University of Vermont. One said: "Look at that guy. Boy! He must have been in a terrible accident!"

The other one said, "Yeah, but ain't that a good-looking suit?"

PHAETON: LEARNING TO DRIVE

Phaeton /fáy-eh-tun/ ("the shining one") son of the Greek Sun God Helios by an Ethiopian virgin.

The boy's playmates teased him about his father. "You don't even have a father. Your mother pulled you out of a lizard's hole!" they laughed. "If you had a father we would see him go to his fields every morning. Or in the square playing dominoes with other fathers."

The boy went home crying to his mother. "Why don't I have a father like other boys?"

"You do have a father."

"Why don't I see him?"

"You do see him, Phaeton, every day. Your father is Helios, the Sun God. He drives the chariot of the sun across the sky every day."

The boy knew his mother would not lie to him about something that important so the next day he rose before dawn and stood in the square to wave as his father rose over the mountains. Again at mid day, he waved. "Hi, papa!" he called. In the evening he stood on the western edge of the village waving, "Goodbye, papa!" His playmates laughed at him again.

He came home with a broken heart. His mother had not told him the truth. This time she said, "If you don't believe me, Phaeton, you're going to have to ask your father."

The next day he began walking toward the East to find his father — from Ethiopia, across the Middle East, down across Persia, across Afghanistan and into India, headed for the farthest most coast of the world where he found the temple of the Sun God high on a mountaintop. He struggled his way to the top where it was so bright he could barely make out a temple with massive pillars holding up the roof. It was always high noon up there. When Helios noticed him he called to him, "Boy ...you out there. What do you want? What are doing up here?"

Shading his eyes as best he could with his hand,

Phaeton called out: "My mother says that my father is Helios, the Sun God. I've come to find him." At that, Helios removed his flaming crown and tucked it behind the throne. "Come in here, boy." Phaeton made his way in and stood before the throne. Helios drew him near to put his arm around him. "Tell me your name."

"Phaeton."

"Now, Phaeton, what's this about me being your father? What is your mother' name?"

When Phaeton told him, Helios smiled at the memory. "Yes, I am your father and I'm proud to say it. You can go and tell that to your playmates."

"But the boys will never believe me," said Phaeton. "I've got to take something back. Something has to happen. If I just say that I saw you, they will ask me for proof."

"Well," said Helios. "You name it — anything you want to take back. Name your heart's desire and you can take it back and show your little friends."

From the moment his mother told him that his father was Helios the Sun God, Phaeton knew in his heart he wanted to drive that chariot across the sky. Wait 'till I go by Ethiopia, he thought, I'll call down to my friends and they'll see me up there. They'll believe me then! He looked up at his father and said, "I want to take your place."

Helios held him out at arm's length. "Exactly what do you mean by that?" he demanded. Phaeton saw that the tenor in the temple had changed and for the worse. In haste he added: "Just for a day; just one day. I want to drive the chariot of the sun across the sky. Just once. One day."

"That's impossible! You can't drive the chariot. It's too big, too heavy, and you're too small. You can't do that!"

"But, you promised."

"Well, I promised, but it was rash of me. You just can't do it," he blustered. "You'll kill yourself. And you'll turn the world on its head!"

Phaeton looked down at his sandals. "All the same," he said, "you did promise."

"Are you testing a father's love? Is that it? Let the evidence of my love be my pleas to abandon this suicidal quest! You may hope you'll go up there to Heaven and find it brimming with gods and goddesses in their temples, everyone drinking wine and eating grapes. Let me set you straight; it's no place for a boy. Don't forget Cancer, the great crab, is up there just waiting for a sweet, tender boy to grab and eat. Taurus the Bull is waiting to crush you under his hoof. Ever been stung by a giant scorpion, son? You're in for a lot of trouble if you get up there and you think it's going to be easy. You make one wrong turn among those unmarked clouds — I have come close to losing the way myself."

"A promise," pouted Phaeton, "is a promise."

"I know I promised but I didn't exactly promise this. Son, there are gods on Mount Olympus who can do anything they want, but not one of them could drive that chariot across the sky. Even Zeus can't drive that chariot! There are times when I get up there,I don't dare look over the side."

Even as they spoke, the hour approached for the sun to rise up out of the Eastern Sea. Helios' minions opened the gates and fit the bejeweled harnesses onto four winged stallions.

The petulant stubbornness of youth had filled the approaching hour until Helios could no longer ignore that when a god makes a promise, whether foolish or wise, he must keep it. The Sun God retrieved his glowing crown and followed his retinue to the stables where he lifted the boy into the chariot. In frustrated surrender Helios spoke to the foolish boy. "If you insist on doing this insane thing, at least let me show you how to drive."

My father taught me to drive right after WWII. No civilian vehicles were made during the War. Car makers were turning out tanks and half-tracks. After the War everyone wanted new wheels. My dad was no exception. What he wanted was a special make — a Packard. I think it was my father's only extravagance, but he wanted that car and he bought it. That's the car I learned to drive on.

Dad would drive us up our brick street, then onto North Main and, at the city limits, we turned onto West Oak Hill Road. West Oak Hill was a farm-to-market road, dirt surfaced, but well maintained — a good place to learn to drive because there wasn't much traffic on it.

Once there I got into the driver's seat and he taught me how to turn, back up, turn on the windshield wipers and shift gears using, of course, the stick shift. He pointed out more than once that the clutch was by my left foot and the brake by my right foot.

One summer afternoon after my lesson my dad said, "I think that's enough for today." I stopped the car, turned off the motor and reached for the door handle when he said, "No, I think today you can drive the car home."

My palms were sweaty as I slid back into the seat and eased slowly down West Oak Hill Road. I drove to the corner of Main Street and looked both ways, not wanting to see any cars coming when I turned onto the busy thoroughfare. Once on Main Street I drove several blocks before turning right again onto Prendergast* Street where our house lay half way down the hill on the left.

As we rolled down the hill my father said, "Tommy, there's one thing you're doing that needs improvement. You're turning into the driveway too soon. As soon you see the driveway, you start turning. You've got to wait until your front wheels are almost even with the driveway then turn a sharp left. If you use the manhole cover to mark your turning point you'll roll up over the sidewalk and right into the driveway. So wait for that spot before you turn."

It was much on my mind as I drove down the street. I turned into the cinder-covered driveway to be met with its reassuring crunch under the tires of that big brand new Packard automobile.

"Two things are vital!" Helios told his son. "Control and Altitude. Never let go of those reins. Hang on at all cost! These stallions will sense that I'm not back there if they can't feel an iron grip on the reins."

*See Notes

171

"Uh huh," said Phaeton without hearing.

Helios pointed at the black whip in its socket on the chariot wall. "Reach me that whip," he said. "These fellows don't need any urging from you — they'll be charging the whole way! You'll need both hands on those reins."

"Uh huh."

Helios shouted now to be heard over the tumult of gates grinding open, horses snorting, hooves clattering the golden cobbles and the shouting of the handlers. "When these horses take off they'll climb straight up. You'll think you're going to fall out of the back. As the horses level off you will see the tracks I made yesterday bearing off to your left. Follow those tracks all the way to the western sea and you'll be all right."

"Uh huh."

Helios' mouth was touching Phaeton's ear to make himself heard. "And altitude!" he shouted. "Drive too low and you'll scorch the earth. Too high and you'll tear the fabric of Heaven. As in all things keep to the middle path."

"Uh huh." Phaeton hadn't heard a word. He anticipated only getting into the sky over Ethiopia.

The horses chomped at their bits, stretching their wing muscles. Helios spread a protective grease over his son's head and shoulders. Without warning a fury of wings bore the horses through the air, their hooves reaching for the heavens. They soared straight up. Almost at once the stallions realized that it wasn't the old man back there and they took off in high spirits plunging left — climbing right — first west — then east. They soared higher — then lower. All the while the boy hung on for dear life!

Tossed from one end of the chariot to the other he soon let go of the reins to better grip the walls of the chariot. It didn't occur to him to look for Ethiopia. His eyes were shut tight. He just wanted to die before anything more happened. Without a driver the horses drew the chariot so high it burned a scar across the bottom of heaven. Those who look up at night can still see that scar. They roared back down and over Ethiopia so close to the earth the chariot burned the people black — Phaeton's mother, his little friends, his aunts and uncles, were all burned black. Ethiopians remain black to this day. The chariot coursed low over the Nile leaving the river boiling behind it. In fear, the river buried its head somewhere in Sudan and to this day has never pulled it out.

High again they went over Italy where mountains exploded to spew lava down their sides. Mountains blew enough ash into the air to bury villagers alive inside their shops and homes. The panicked horses plunged south where, swooping across the Great Sahara rainforest, the sun consumed every leaf, every twig, every limb, every trunk, every root.

In a panic Demeter, the goddess of nature, called on Zeus to do something. "That boy is taking us back to the beginning of time, back to chaos! We'll have to start from scratch!" Zeus reached for his quiver of thunderbolts. Hoisting one of them overhead, he took aim on the wayward chariot.

Now, I have to confess that I didn't so much want to learn how to drive — driving wasn't all that important to me. What was important to me was being seen driving. To be seen driving by my neighborhood pals: Jack, Junior, Margaret and especially by Mary Olson who lived in the house next door. From the driveway Mary Olson's porch was up there on my left just past the concrete retaining wall. I pictured Mary Olson looking down from her porch glider and saying, "Well, there's Tommy Weakley. He's driving a Packard automobile. Maybe I shouldn't have been laughing at him all these years." As I made that left-hand turn I allowed myself a glance toward her porch without noting our gradual drift toward that concrete wall with this brand … new …Packard …automobile. My father yelled: "Brake! Brake! Hit the brake!"

I panicked, jamming my left foot down onto the clutch as hard as I could (thereby disengaging everything) allowing us to slide along that wall …scraping, crunching, grinding. Then, because I didn't know what else to do I took my foot off the "brake." As I did, of course, the car shook with the spasm of the stall, first grinding upward then screeching downward against the wall.

I sat there next to my father awaiting a thunderbolt.

Zeus' thunderbolt smashed that chariot to smithereens. The horses, now free, plunged down, clawing their way into the depths of the Mediterranean. The boy, his hair now blazing afire, arched through the sky like a shooting star before falling into the River Po.

Phaeton's sisters came to stand on the banks of the river, mourning the loss of this foolish boy and grieving so long that they took root. They became aspen trees. Every autumn they cry all over again, their golden tears falling into the Po as it carries the leaves to the sea.

I sat shaking in the driver's seat, head down awaiting judgment. My father said, "Back away."

I started the car and backed away to suffer the withdrawal of the bumper, the fender, the running board, everything grinding along the cement wall. I worked the car out into the driveway, turned off the key. We sat there in silence. Instead of a thunderbolt I got a pat on the knee. My father said, "Tommy, for the rest of your life you'll know the difference between the clutch pedal and the brake pedal."

It would be hard to find a man who hasn't spent much of his life waiting for his father to tell him he loves him. My father didn't say those words either that day. But I knew what it meant when he squeezed my knee.

THE NEW YORK BLUEPRINT

The Blue Benn Diner in Bennington has been an institution since 1942, offering a large menu of vegetarian fare as well as hearty diner staples. It has never been enlarged which means you often wait for a booth. They'll let a single patron sit at one, but they like it better if you opt for a counter seat. Clientele is as mixed as the menu suggests: both blue and white collars, professional people, college kids, tourists, bikers, the gray-haired, the no-haired and anyone who likes company with their food.

One morning not long ago John Davies* and I sat at the counter when an argument in one of the booths drew our attention. Two men were sitting face to face with blueprints spread on the table between them. I recognized the older man as a local builder. From

*See Notes

their conversation I gathered that the younger man, in coat and tie, was from out of state. It became apparent he had bought a piece of Vermont mountain-view property and planned to build a summer home on it. The local builder was annoyed that the New Yorker (it turned out) insisted on using the blueprints he had brought with him.

The local builder dismissed them with a wave of the hand. "Those blueprints you got aren't worth a damn! Fellow drew up those prints didn't know a thing about building houses."

"Well," said the New Yorker, "they were drawn up by the finest architectural firm in New York City. Fella that drew them up has been here; he's stood on the ground; he knows what he's doing."

"No," said the builder, "I don't care. This is all screwed up. You ought to get some local fella' to make you a new set of prints."

The landowner got to his feet and began rolling up the papers. "I'm still going to use these blueprints. I like what he's designed; we worked together on it. If you can't do it, I'm going to find me another builder."

The builder stood up. "All right!" he said. "I'll build the damn house, but I'll tell you this. You use those blueprints — you're gonna end up with two bathrooms!"

CHRISTMAS IN PARADISE

I was twelve years old the second of December of 1941 when my mother's Great-Aunt Florence had a massive heart attack at the top of the stone steps of Saints Peter and Paul Catholic Church and was dead before she hit the bottom stair.

I didn't know a lot about mother's Great-Aunt Florence. All I had was incidental intelligence, picked up at the dinner table. One thing stood out. Great-Aunt Florence was the only Catholic in our whole family. She was Catholic because she and a young man by the name of Peterson fell in love and Mr. Peterson's family wouldn't let him marry somebody who wasn't

Catholic. Florence loved him so much that she became Catholic. She did everything necessary: bought a Catholic Bible, studied the courses, the interviews, maybe even Catechism, I don't know, until she became a Catholic. Or, as my father said, Florence turned.

But they never did get married because he went off to fight a war in Cuba and came back in a wooden box. Though I never saw it, mother told us that, often when she went to see her, Aunt Florence would go over to her piano and pick up the picture of Mr. Peterson in his uniform. With the cuff of her sleeve she would wipe off the glass. She'd get weepy and say, "Oh, Ethel, I hope I don't live to see another war."

After Mr. Peterson came home in a box people in the family expected her to come to her senses and return to the Methodist Church. She didn't. She told mother she was going to keep the faith.

According to my father Florence was "a bit of a tippler." She didn't tipple a lot, but she tippled regular. She would have a little glass of port every night before she went to bed. "To settle her stomach," my mother explained.

For an old lady, she subscribed to some interesting magazines. She subscribed to *True Confessions*, for instance. And *True Romance*. Those magazines didn't have any currency in our house, except that sometimes Florence would press a copy on my mother and say,

"Oh, Ethel, this is so beautiful, you've got to read this story." Mother dutifully brought the magazine home. I don't know if she ever read the stories or not. My dad got *True Detective* magazine. He read all those stories.

And Florence did all kinds of needlework. She knitted things for Catholic bazaars. She made aprons and crib quilts and all manner of pot holders. She stuffed little pillows with balsam needles, she made baby clothes and did crochet work. But it was her embroidery that brought grief to our house.

She took it upon herself every Christmas to give us a gift of a handkerchief, all three of us kids. There was Miriam, the oldest, then Jeanne, the middle child. Then there was me. Every Christmas we each received a hankie. We saw them there under the Christmas tree. We avoided them like brussels sprouts. When all the other gifts had been opened, they'd be lying there on the floor, wrapped in cheap, white tissue paper, held together with Christmas Seals from the American Tuberculosis Society. Pick one up and it went limp in your fingers.

The girls' hankies were embroidered in one corner — maybe a wreath with red berries on it or a bluebird or an angel or the like. I got initials - TW I got, sometimes just W. The worst part was that mother made us write thank you notes for these things on Christmas Day.

"You've got to," she said. "That note has to be written, put in an envelope, sealed, addressed, stamped and put in the mailbox today. If you put it off it will be January and a whole year before she gets a thank you note." Which was most likely true.

I tried bargaining — one year I suggested that I do the envelope business and put the hankie in the envelope and write "thank you" and send it back. That earned me a crack across the behind with a rolled up newspaper. My mother said, "It's not the hankie. You're really not thanking her for the hankie, it's the love she puts into it. You're thanking her for choosing this way to tell you she loves you. It's not easy for her."

"She has a funny way of telling us," I said.

So, there it was — December — and God, in His infinite wisdom, had seen fit to give Great-Aunt Florence a massive heart attack at the top of the stone steps at the Saints Peter and Paul Catholic Church and she was dead before she hit the bottom. So I didn't have to write a letter that year, because Great-Aunt Florence was spending Christmas in Paradise.

The viewing was held downtown at the Partridge Funeral Home. My older sisters didn't want to go. "Do we have to go? It's so boring. It'll be nothing but old people. We'll have to hang around waiting for you."

"You've got to come," Mother told them. "We

have to show support for Aunt Florence. There aren't going to be many others there." For my part, I looked forward to going. I had never seen a dead person and I wanted to see what a dead person looked like.

All the way downtown Mother complained as she did every year about the merchants. "Here it is, only the fifth of the month," she said, "and all the decorations are up."

We got to the funeral home, took our coats off and a white-haired old man escorted my mother and father up to the casket. My father whispered, "Florence does not look like an 85-year-old woman who has pitched headfirst down the stone steps of Saints Peter and Paul Catholic Church." When they came away to mingle with the few other people there, it was time for us kids to go up.

The three of us advanced on the casket. There, in front of it, Mr. Partridge had placed a little step stool so that shorter mourners like me could see down into the casket. It had a handle on the side to help me mount the padded step. I had no sooner focused my gaze on the remains of the old lady when my sister Miriam's hand grabbed my arm. "Get off there," she said, "that's for Catholics!"

So I stood on tiptoes. It didn't take long to satisfy my curiosity and I made my way to the folding chairs against the walls to wait wondering when we'd be going home. Just then my mother came in through the front door again, this time without her coat. She'd gone back to the car for something. She crossed the room carrying a framed picture of a man in uniform. Heading for the casket she pulled down the cuff of her dress with which she wiped the glass. Turning it until Mr. Peterson faced Great-Aunt Florence's head, she slid it down between the satin lining of the casket and the pillow on which Aunt Florence's head rested. I was intrigued.

On the way home through the snowy streets I called up from my place in the middle of the back seat, "Mother, are you going to leave that picture in the casket when Aunt Florence is buried?"

Over her shoulder she said, "Yes I am, I'm sending the picture of Mr. Peterson to heaven with Aunt Florence."

That opened up a world of possibilities. "Well," I said, "would it be all right if the three of us put something in the casket to go to heaven with Great-Aunt Florence?"

"No!" she said. "That would be an imposition on Mr. Partridge. It would complicate his job."

My father, who was up front negotiating the snowy roads, said, "Now, Ethel, just think about it a minute. What could be the harm in it? If it wasn't something that was big and stuck out, I don't imagine

Mr. Partridge would mind."

Well, they talked it back and forth. Finally my mother, with a shrug, said, "Well, all right, you can do it — but no hankies!"

So, on to Plan B.

From the beginning I thought my older sisters would think it was corny, but they kind of liked the idea. So, Saturday morning, the day of the funeral, found the three of us fanning out across downtown Jamestown looking for something to send to Paradise with Great-Aunt Florence. I headed straight for the Humidor on the corner of Third and Spring streets, where my dad bought his Raleigh cigarettes. I went in and headed straight for the magazine rack to seek out *True Romance*, pulling up the December issue. Wait! I thought, maybe she's already seen this copy and, besides, the couple on the cover of *True Romance* were sitting on the davenport looking at each other in such a way that I figured sooner or later they would wind up on the cover of *True Confessions*. I stepped to another rack looking for something that would be acceptable to all the nuns who would be looking over Great-Aunt Florence's shoulder in Catholic heaven.

It was a given for me that Catholics had their own heaven. Didn't they, after all, have their own cemetery? Not to mention their own Bible. Their own language.

I made my way over to the magazines that were

more familiar to me — the comics. Now, my comic of choice when I was twelve years old was Captain Marvel. The reason I liked Captain Marvel especially was that at the beginning of every story he was a boy. He was a boy like me and when he would see a wrong that needed righting, he would say the magic word, which was — "SHAZAM!" — and this lightning bolt would come down from heaven, strike him smack on top of his head and turn him into Captain Marvel. It beefed him up, changed his clothes and everything! And I thought that would be swell, particularly because Shazam sounded like a Catholic word to me. I thought when the fellow comes down the aisle swinging the smoky thing he could easily be chanting "shazam... shazam... shazam." It would fit right in.

I was close to pulling it out of the rack when I imagined my mother's voice saying, "What have you got there?"

Captain Marvel would never pass muster with my mother.

I moved on to another section of comics — what parents called good comics: Little Lulu, Henry, Archie and His Friends. Never catch me reading one of those. I moved over again and found the perfect thing — Classic Comics. Classic Comics were still comic books; they had four-color drawings in panels and all their dialogue in balloons over people's heads, but the stories were all from classic literature. It might be an abridgment of, say, *Treasure Island* or *Robinson Crusoe*, *Kidnapped*, *Last of the Mohicans* or something like that. No grownup ever objected to kids reading one those.

Classic Comics were the kind you would find rolled up in your stocking on Christmas morning taking up perfectly good space where a slingshot could have fit.

Well, this issue was the story of Sir Gawain and the Lady Ragnell. The cover showed a knight and a castle and a beautiful princess. I figured, "This is as close to *True Romance* as I'll get," so I pulled it out, ran over to the register, put my dime on the counter and went out with the book.

Saturday afternoon at the funeral home, the three of us gathered to put our things in the casket to go to Paradise with Great-Aunt Florence. My sister Miriam, the oldest, the only one old enough to be able to do this, had gone to a liquor store to buy an eight-ounce bottle of port wine, made in England. Had a black label on it that I thought fitting for the occasion. She tucked the bottle next to the picture. Then I took my rolled up comic of Sir Gawain and the Lady Ragnell to lay next to the picture.

What Jeanne, the middle child, brought to the casket that day I wish I had thought of myself. She had gone down to Bigelow's Department Store, into the notions department, and had bought a hank of embroidery floss in a shade of blue that I called "virgin blue." It was the color of the Virgin Mother's shawl in all the classic paintings of the Nativity.

Jeanne held it out for mother to see. "Is it okay," she said, "if I put this in Aunt Florence's hand? It could get lost otherwise."

"Yes," mother said, "but don't disturb the crucifix in her hand." Jeanne stood beside the casket to lift one of Aunt Florence's hands to lay that slender hank of embroidery floss in place and put the hand down again.

It did not escape my attention that my sister had just touched a dead person. Now I wanted to touch a dead person. I said to mother, "Would it be okay if I touched Great-Aunt Florence's hand the way Jeanne did?" invoking Jeanne's name to make it a fairness issue.

Mother sighed, "Yes, that's all right, you can touch her hand." I walked back to the casket, carefully avoiding the little stool for short Catholics. I stretched to lay my warm hand on top of Great-Aunt Florence's cold hand. At that moment I learned something about Aunt Florence that I had never known.

When I took my hand away I peered into the casket to confirm what my hand had just told me. Her knuckles were the size of walnuts. Her fingers were twisted, gnarled together. They looked like five pieces of clothesline tied together and tossed out in a freezing rain. I knew then what my mother meant every

Christmas when she told us, "It's not the hankies, it's the love she puts into the hankies." What must have gone into making the letter "W" with fingers that crippled, I wondered.

After the funeral and extended goodbyes we spattered our way home through the slush to our traditional Saturday night supper: Campbell's tomato soup and grilled cheese sandwich. We listened to the Jimmy Durante show. I went upstairs, got into bed and turned out the lights. I lay there picturing Great-Aunt Florence in her rocking chair on her first night in Paradise.

She was embroidering using the virgin-blue floss that my sister had given her. The Holy Mother passed by on her way to chapel only to realize she had forgotten her hat …and she had no veil.

"I'll just have to go back," Mary said.

"There's no need," Florence told her. "I've just finished this handkerchief. Use it to cover your head."

Every so often Great-Aunt Florence reached over to a little table and her small bottle of port wine. She took a little nip of it. And because it was Paradise, the bottle never emptied. Then she moistened the end of a finger to turn a page in Classic Comics, reading about Sir Gawain and how he had kept faith with the Lady Ragnell. She rested in the understanding that, just like Gawain, she had kept faith with Mr. Peterson and that hers, like Gawain's, was a true romance.

Then I turned over, shut my eyes, burrowed under the covers and went to sleep. It was Saturday night, December 6, 1941.

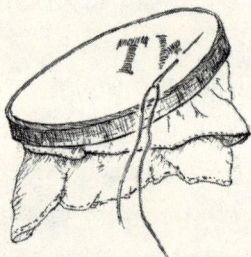

SETTLERS

A long time ago, before storytellers, there was nothing — a void. But God got lonely and sought companionship. He reached into that void and he pulled away parts of it. He formed it into a ball and threw it up in the air. He named it Earth after his mother. The ball wasn't enough company; he was still lonely. He tore out some clay from different parts of Earth. He shaped it, rolled the pieces between his hands and when the sun had dried them he breathed on them and they came alive. He came down to talk to them.

"What I want you to do," he told them, "is go around the world and multiply. I'll pick out places for you."

"So," he says, "how many people here like to cook?" Hands went up and he sent all those people to France.

Some people were standing there shivering. He sent all those people to Equatorial Africa. Others were sweating. He sent them all up to Hudson Bay. Some of his choices were no-brainers. If you looked Chinese, he sent you to China. If he caught you arguing, he sent you to Israel.

"Go multiply," he told them," all over the world so that when I come back I won't be lonely." He turned to go, only to find a group of people standing there. "What are you doing here?" he asked.

"Well," they said, "you haven't told us where to go."

"Why didn't you speak up before I gave everything away?"

"We are not people who put ourselves forward," said one man.

"And we don't give unasked for advice," added another.

"I wish you had spoken up," said God. "There's just one place left on Earth and I was saving that for myself, but now you'll have to have it."

And that's how Vermont got its first settlers.

Notes to Stories

TWO PICKPOCKETS. Collected in Manchester, England, by Katharine Briggs for her book "British Folk Tales". First told by Tom in a warm-up exercise in the first Jeannine Laverty storytelling workshop he attended the fall of 1981. Recorded in 1991 on CD titled *Tom Weakley, RFD Vermont*, now out of print.

ADRIFT ON THE ALFALFA SEA. Written in February 1986 for a winter storytelling workshop. Not recorded.

SLEEPING OUTSIDE EDEN. Written August 1988 for a summer storytelling workshop. Not recorded.

THE RASPBERRY AFFAIR. Recorded September 1991 under the title *Waiting on the Lord* on CD titled *Tom Weakley, RFD Vermont*, now out of print.

DIRECTIONS. Recorded 2001 on the CD titled *Breakfast at the Blue Benn Diner.*

THE METHODIST COMMUNION. Recorded 1991 on CD titled *Tom Weakley, RFD Vermont,* now out of print.

TOMMY. Recorded 1992 on CD titled *Harry and the Texaco Boys,* now out of print. The manner in which Tommy's mother calls him and in which he responds is known musically as the descending *minor third melodic interval* — two notes, the second lower than the first.

This is the first music children learn on the streets around the world. The *nyah nyah* taunt uses it. It's the sound of the first word in *Frosty the Snowman.* Historically it is associated with sadness, as in the waning autumnal notes of the katydids in *Esther.*

MISTER FURLONG. Recorded 1992 on CD titled *Harry and the Texaco Boys,* now out of print.

DO YOU LOVE ME, MARY OLSON. Recorded 1992 on CD titled *Harry and the Texaco Boys,* now out of print.

Also on a two-CD set titled *An Evening with Tom Weakley* recorded March 2008 at Tom's retirement performance at the Caffè Lena, Saratoga Springs, NY.

COUNTRY BOY. Written March 1992. Not recorded.

ESTHER. Begun around 1997; stopped revising in 2012. Not recorded.

THE 7:02 TRAIN TO BELLOWS FALLS. Recorded 2001 on CD titled *Breakfast at the Blue Benn Diner.*

THE MAN WHO CLUNG TO EARTH. Recorded September 1994 on CD titled *White Mules and Hoop Snakes.* Out of print. Adapted from a Cretan story related by William J. Bausch in his book *Storytelling: Imagination and Faith.*

DEER EYES, A DRAMA. Recorded 1994 as a monologue on CD titled *Breakfast at the Blue Benn Diner.* The monologue version didn't read well in print, thus a drama version.

THE BAKED BEANS. Recorded September 1994 on a CD titled *White Mules & Hoop Snakes.* Now out of print.

THE GOOD LOOKIN' SUIT was recorded on the two-CD set *An Evening With Tom Weakley* recorded March 2008 at Tom's retirement performance at Caffè Lena in Saratoga, NY. It's my belief this was an old vaudeville staple.

PHAETON: LEARNING TO DRIVE. Recorded March 2008 on a two-CD set titled *An Evening with Tom Weakley* recorded at Tom's retirement performance at Caffè Lena, Saratoga Springs, NY.

THE NEW YORK BLUEPRINT. Recorded 2001 on CD titled *Breakfast at the Blue Benn Diner.* Master Builder John Davies laughed so hard at this that I added him to the story.

CHRISTMAS IN PARADISE. Recorded 2004 on CD titled *Christmas in Paradise.* Also recorded March 2008 on two-CD set titled *An Evening With Tom Weakley* recorded at Tom's retirement performance at Caffè Lena, Saratoga Springs, NY.

SETTLERS. Recorded 2001 on CD titled *Breakfast at the Blue Benn Diner.*

OTHER WORKS BY TOM WEAKLEY

1991   TOM WEAKLEY, RFD, VERMONT CD

1992   HARRY AND THE TEXACO BOYS CD

1994   WHITE MULES AND HOOP SNAKES CD

2001   BREAKFAST AT THE BLUE BENN DINER   CD *

2002   REBELS IN VERMONT CD

2004   CHRISTMAS IN PARADISE CD *

2008   AN EVENING WITH TOM WEAKLEY, SET OF TWO CDS *

Still in print